TAILOR MADE

James Brock

TAILOR MADE

Beau to Beau Books
Celebrations of Male Love
E-mail: info@beautobeau.com
Website: http://www.beautobeau.com
ISBN: 978-1-61845-077-7
Printed in the United States of America
For additional copies, please e-mail us at
info@beautobeau.com

"*I really don't remember much about the making of Cleopatra.*

There was a lot of other stuff going on."

Elizabeth Taylor

For Candace Taylor, the sister of my heart

And

Bill Bowen

ONE

"God I hope I get it, I hope I get it…"

I hate it when a song gets stuck in my head, especially when I'm trying to concentrate. I wasn't only trying to focus, though. I was also trying to grow three inches and change the color of my hair mentally. The thoughts weren't working though, my 'do remained mouse brown while every other guy in the room actually seemed to be getting blonder. As if being an eight foot tall model hot Scandinavian wasn't enough, they all probably had a degree from an Ivy League school and could unhinge their jaws like an anaconda.

I have a degree but not from a fancy school, and am no more sexually exotic than Mary Poppins. If the wealth of information I have given you about me: brown hair, mediocre education, limited jaw dropping ability, doesn't at least make you curious about where I was sitting, then you are just not using your imagination.

The song buzzing in my brain was from the Tony/Pulitzer/Emmy/Grammy/Oscar/Nobel (well if it wasn't at least nominated for some of those it should have been-show tune loving, another "me" attribute-peeling myself like the layers of an onion huh!) award winning musical *Chorus Line*. The words had been ringing in my ear for two weeks, or since a bartender bud of mine had clued me in that a job was being interviewed for today and had even pulled a string (or sucked a few things-he liked me what can I say) or three to get me a spot in the beautifully appointed room I was seated in.

More stuff about me! I seem to be unemployed! You should also know that in addition to being TALL, the other guys I was in the room with were porn star attractive. Seriously, if they didn't get hired (which was certainly MY hope) there were enough of them to keep Chi Chi LaRue in models for a long while.

Two words best describe my situation: economic downturn. I had been part of the fat trimmed from a banking industry middle management position that consisted of typing, filing, and a lot of interoffice romance and birthday cake in the break room and was frankly getting just a little desperate. Unemployment was about to run out and I was soon to move out of the apartment lovingly decorated by me and my lying, cheating filthy whore of an ex boyfriend.

Not long ago I had walked into our cozy little home sweet home to find him drilling my (NOW FORMER) best friend like he expected to hit a vein of diamonds in his lower intestine.

Words (should be needless to say) were said loudly. Ob'jet d'art throw! Well ob'jet d'Ikea, we were pretty budget restricted. Screams! Curses! Crying! The gamut of emotion: rage to denial to acceptance played out in our former little love nest. Loud unsavory behavior went on for quite some time, seemed like it went on for days, but it was probably only hours. The neighbors, I am certain, could give you an exact account of the time as can the PPD, Portland Police Department, who sent some very patient officers to tell us to *knock it the fudge off.*

Which we did because we were STUCK living together until the lease ended or we would not get our (substantial!) deposit back. At that time he (the now ex) and the lying, filthy cheater (former bestie) would go make their own love cocoon. While it made financial sense for me to stay there, it was also sheer hell having that OTHER WHORE there all of the time now, the two of them billing and cooing – all but grooming one another like baboons.

Which made Love become a four letter word I would not be using for some time. A lone wolf out to howl, that would be me. I'd use another four letter word, Done, in place of Love. Besides, I wasn't ever really in *love* with him, the kind of love that made him a deep fascination. Knowing that he hated cilantro and adored Katy Perry should have been *World Almanac* style pieces of information I held onto like bits of pirate treasure in those long agonizing moments when we were apart. Like when we were at a party and he was in the bathroom. I should have had those memories to reflect on to tide me over until he got back, using them to keep him fresh because I couldn't/didn't want to live without him. Instead, I usually just had another drink and scoped out hot guys, so yeah, I may have been in very deep like with the guy but I wasn't truly in love with him.

Or so I told myself.

I did want to be in love again someday but I had bigger stuff going on by then.

Like the plagues of Job, I got canned right about then. While the clowns I was forced to live with were eating high on the hog at IHop and Denny's (pretty classy joints for my income by then), I was shopping at the broken food store. You know, the chain where food that is just about to go back is sold at a discount. No complaining, though, and I was happy to live close enough to one I could walk to. Yeah, there was that ONE incident with the salmon that took me down for three days but c'mon, discount seafood means rolling the dice on salmonella every time.

So yeah, life had taken some turns that I need to explain, so please just have some patience as I AM getting back to the interview and waiting room and no, I wasn't interviewing for work in the porn industry.

Although.

Yes, I did some porn.

More reveal!

I was in college and broke and well, it was a good offer for fast money and I was hungry, well thirsty. I needed beer $$$ and was not picky about where it came from. A guy approached me one afternoon and asked if I would do a quick solo movie. The money he offered was great and I was in a room with just myself, a hot porno playing and a camera rolling. I churned one out faster than it takes to make butter, was paid and on my way after giving the guy my number. He called again a short time later and doubled the offer if I would do a duo, which turned into a trio, which turned into doing stuff with guys I would have PAID to do stuff with, and the next thing you know, what had just been a fun hobby (yeah, sex, I was young and having fun) had turned into a profitable little career.

Okay, another quick detour for more reveal (getting to know me pretty quick, huh!), if you did not question the combination of "Ivy league degree/unhinge jaw like Anaconda", then you SHOULD at least have questioned how a guy my age in this day and age would know how butter is made.

Simple. I was raised on a working farm far, far inland from the beautiful Oregon coast. And by working farm I mean cows and pigs and alfalfa growing and school tours and all that comes with the, well, work that goes on, on a working farm. Three brothers and a sister and we all know how to shear sheep and spin wool and milk cows and goats and yup, churn that butter!

And I hated every clip, spin, squirt and plunge of the handle. I LOVE my family but detested the farm, the working farm my parents and brothers still run. My sister married a guy and moved to Salem while I ran to the bright lights of the city as soon as I graduated college with that degree. And in that beautiful little jewel of a city (Portland, Oregon) I found the perfect jewel of a guy and we settled in together and, well, you already know how THAT has ended. The ex (remember? Filthy Lying Whore?) did not know about my moment on the silver (ish, and for movies like I was in semen splattered) screen but during a fun if drunken evening partying with my former best friend – the OTHER filthy lying whore in this story (so far….) – I had shown him a DVD of my work. So of course by now the ex knew and, believe me, he drug THAT little episode of my past up at least once during every little argument, which were happening now on a regular basis.

But if I am anything, I am a bounce back kinda guy. Like when the guy I filmed my first porn with and I finished, the "director" – well the guy aiming the camera at us – thanked and paid us, we did not discuss the moral implication of what we had just done. We took the (easy) money, bought more beer and some substances not sold in pharmaceutical stores, and shagged back to my filthy little dorm room where we stripped off again and fucked like bunnies for the next two days. Wish I had made a DVD of THAT little encounter, would have made enough to have not been sitting here for this interview now, but if wishes were horses, beggars would ride, as one of my wise family members said some ten BILLION times during my childhood. The same one (of two parents, that is) who remind me every time I am in touch with home that there is a tractor in the barn with my name on it. It is nice to have that as a fall back, but I have made a vow that I will join the priesthood or do porn until my balls drag the ground before I will ever go back to tilling that sacred soil which has been in my family since about the time Lewis and Clark popped up over yonder hillside looking for the Pacific ocean. Or so family lore goes. If the porn story ever gets out, they will bring in an arborist to prune my branch from the family tree. Not because of that one or two movies, though, but perhaps because of the five or nine or twenty-six that followed. Yeah, I made quite a local name for myself in that industry. Hey, it paid the bills, didn't hurt anyone and I was never sexually unsatisfied, so life was pretty good. I frequently was recognized in clubs, got comp drinks and was constantly hit on by cute guys and drug dealers who wanted me to be the spokes model for their particular line. Never, thankfully, did I get too involved in those operations, though. Then I met that man of my dreams and we moved in together and there was that talk of adopting a rescue dog so I nailed my last slut on film (I know, I know-*pot calling kettle* on that...) and took that job in the bank, putting the glamour and lube filled world of show business behind me.

And we, of course, know how THAT turned out – me dumped by both relationship and job while my now ex adopted the slutty former best friend.

So yeah, I am single, canned, nearly homeless and waiting with the group of male swans (ganders, btw – see some farm stuff I learned as a kid translates to city living) to be evaluated on my body of work. I'd much prefer just to be evaluated on my body because despite the fact that I have been recently DUMPED, those abs are still cut.

I knew there would be a line for the job. Hell, there is a line around the block for part time work at Sears these days, but I didn't expect the calendar material guys I would be up against. And trust me, I would like to be up against any of these guys in any other way, save for this one. I was probably the least qualified there and certain I was the only one there because of a bartender. Hey, I gotta go somewhere to get outa the apartment with Tweedles Dee and Dum always there lurking about. They might as well have become attached at the hip for all of the time they spent together. The 'tender I am friendly with, okay, tricked with, and I have come to like each other not just as occasional fuck buddies but as friend-with-benefits even if he is involved with someone. Okay, okay, so the other two are not the only whorish ones in this story, but it is MY story, so don't throw stones and the bartender's relationship is an open(ish) one. Anyway, my 'tender friend got the particulars on the job from his partner, the open spot was as an executive administrative assistant, which sounded suspiciously like a glorified "gopher" to me, but a job is a job, right? And I once-upon-a-time had a childhood career shoveling goat, cow, pig and horse crap. So no complaints from me even if they hand me a shovel right after the words "You're hired!" are spoken.

With only that vague title for the work I am applying for, I am sitting in that impressive and intimidating lobby in a downtown high rise building that has a doorman, rich dark wood paneling (which sets those blond heads around me off stunningly), leather furniture and leather bound books in custom built cases that line the walls. People are probably paid to come in and read them. I feel like I have wandered into an exclusive club of which I am not a member. A feeling I have to shake off, resolving to be confidant, to trust my ability to LAND ON MY FEET and know that if this does not pan out, stone soup is next on my menu line up. Remember that story? Instead of bemoaning the fact that they have no food, this guy starts boiling up a pot of water and drops in a rock. Everyone comes up with a liiiiitttttle something to add to the water and pretty soon a feast is spread and everyone is full and happy. All good in concept but when it came to chow time, the crowd I tended to hang with would pull the stone out of the pot, use it to bop me on the head and when I was down go through my pockets to make certain I wasn't holding out any choice morsels. I needed the job and a better class of friends.

A frosty receptionist with a voice as soft as that of Elizabeth Taylor calls a name. Unlike the late icon, this woman was fighting ageing as if they were in a cage match; her jet black hair was pulled back in

JAMES BROCK   18

a severe cut, skin pulled tight over her face like she was staring down a wind machine, and she was dressed like a teenage hooker. She was as out of place in the quiet, refined office as a clown at a wedding.

While she didn't exactly fit the corporate mold, she must either do an amazing job or have dirt on the boss, I decided. She was pretty and scary at the same time, possibly in her late thirties; she was broad shouldered; even seated I could tell she was tall and that she was probably mistaken for a drag queen on a regular basis.

I liked her immediately.

"Wyatt Taylor. Mr. Bowen will see you now."

That being me, I stood, and realizing my suit had actually wrinkled since sitting down, I felt like I had just rolled out of a dumpster. While hard around the edges, the receptionist looked as if she had been ironed and seemed to sneer at me like I was a pile of dog doo her Louboton had just missed. All that hate directed at me despite the fact that I had just mentally made her my friend. Smiling, I tried to keep my lips from contorting into a grimace that would make me look way demented.

On my feet, canvas courier bag slung over my shoulder making me look like a messenger instead of a hip young potential executive assistant, I took a breath and followed her through a door that looked like it was taken off the hinges of a palace.

I handed the receptionist the (porn free!) resume I had sweated over and printed out on linen paper. I might as well have handed her a piece of paper grocery bag written in crayon for the way she scanned it, then turned and crisply slid it onto a massive desk.

Taking a deep breath, I put my best face on.

Mr. Bowen was on the telephone, not lifting his head or standing as we walked in, the receptionist leaving without a look back.

While my potential new employer, and from the brief glance I had gotten, NEW HUSBAND material, hubba hubba he was a hottie, continued to talk, I took the opportunity to give him a good look over.

Because he was seated I had no way of telling how tall he was but he had big hands (big good looking hands....) and if I squinted I could easily compare him to JFK Jr. with his slight Roman nose, full perfectly formed lips, a thick head of unruly chestnut brown hair....yeah, I was sporting a little wood by then, no lie. I could go on and on about how hot he was making me but just trust me, you would have wanted to be across the desk from him, too.

Of course, you could not live in Portland for even ten minutes without knowing who William

Bowen was. The Bowen Corporation sponsored everything in the city from parades to youth programs; ancestry traced them back to the city founders, in fact. They were so well known that even I knew about Bowen, even if I didn't know exactly what they did.

When the hot man behind the desk did finally glance up at me, I felt the bore of his midnight blue eyes go through to my soul. He was so hot I wished I had listed sucking a gold ball through a garden hose under *Special Skillz*.

"I do not care. Get it done." His voice was deep and modulated, the words spoken in the tone of an emperor making a decree. Clicking the phone off, the executive looked me dead in the eye, and we held a stare for a beat before he broke it. Looking down at the desk, he scanned my resume in a way that made me know he had caught all of the major points and knew my economic situation as well as where I had been born and raised and that I was bargain barn socks and low end Macy's underwear.

In other words, the hottie sitting across from me, who looked to be only a few years older than my own twenty three years, knew how to size someone up.

"Do you have any idea what this position entails?" he serves, a smirk on his lips.

"Executive assisting," I volley.

Bowen grins slightly. "You will be my aide on both the professional and personal level. Nights, weekends. You are on call twenty-four hours a day, seven days a week."

He wants me to fail.

I want to eat.

"There is travel involved."

As long as it isn't time travel, I think, but do not say. I respond to the verbal part of the program with: "I don't have anything to hold me down. Dog, cat, partner." This guy was no stoop, so I had just let him in on my orientation and did not care if he was into guys, girls or geese as long as his checks cleared.

Bowen nodded in a very noncommittal way and took another phone call unrelated to the conversation we were in the middle of.

When he finished the call, Mr. Bowen again scanned my resume and asked if I minded filing. I said no. He then asked about word processing skills, and I told him I could process with the best of them. He asked if I could pass a drug and background check. I said yes, which was at least true for the background check. I had never even had a ticket and hoped my bartender buddy could come up with a little something to help me pass a drug test 'cause it was gonna take a few hours to get my system cleaned out. Nothing major mind you, but I did NOT have glaucoma and that would be the only explanation for what they might find in me right about then. I would have learned Russian or how to make a chocolate soufflé for the job.

Bowen didn't seem to react no matter what I said I could or could not do, so I saw no reason to suggest that I planned on updating my special skills for him.

When the verbal portion of the interview seemed to have come to an end, I stood again and leaned across the desk to shake his offered hand. The skin was soft and conditioned, grip firm. A few strong pumps, then release, much like a good jack off.

Sorry, add "tends to sexualize the most innocent of action" to the "getting to know you" list of me.

"Thank you for taking the time to speak with me, Mr. Bowen."

"You are very welcome, Wynn. Thank you for coming in. How tall are you, by the way?"

Probably illegal for him to ask me that but you know me well enough (well you DO…) to know that it would take a lot more than that for him to shake me. And yeah, he called me Wynn instead of Wyatt but I would cross that bridge if I were hired. He could call me Dolly or Hirem then and I would not care.

"Five nine and a half," I said. I'd added the half inch just in case "tall" was one of the unspoken job requirements. If it was, I was screwed because it was pretty clear all the blonds waiting were over six foot. His smile opened up just enough for me to think I'd made that requirement somehow. Turning, I left the room, stepping back into the waiting area where the sea of towering blond heads swiveled in my direction in unison. Adopting an attitude that I had nailed the interview and been offered the job even though I was walking out still not even knowing what Bowen Industries made, sold, bought or did. Widgets? Sprockets? Baseball diamonds? I didn't care (as you well know), but the attitude worked and I saw several of the blonds slowly slump back down into their seats.

"Mr. Bowen will be making a decision soon and we will let you know either way," the receptionist said, nearly without looking up from her computer screen. Leaning in, SHE then scanned me up and down, then continued. "Mr. Bowen doesn't like to be kept waiting so keep your phone handy." This was said in a long hiss of breath in an undertone. She gave a fast glance around the room as if to see if any of the other candidates had been listening, then darted her eyes back to her computer screen. I did fall off a turnip truck but it had been a few years since then and I had learned a few things, like when I had been dismissed.

With that, I left the suite, took the elevator back to the lobby and just like that I was back in my own life. Which as you know does not take us any place special or fun. The rest of the afternoon stretched out in front of me like a blank page. The monkey butt twins were back at the apartment so I did NOT want to go back there. I had no job to go to, no money for shopping, so the only thing left to do was go drink. Well, I could have found an orphanage and done some volunteer work or bathed someone homeless or some other such good work, but I've copped enough of the true parts of me that you know that is not how I roll.

So I scooted on through town to where the gay bars are popped into one, loosening my tie as I passed through the doorway.

The cute 'tender on duty was my buddy. I guess my smile gave away that I thought I had a good interview but I was grinning because he is smokin' hot and it was Friday and he was just standing there looking hot polishing a glass. I slid onto a stool on the civilian side of the bar as he pushed a cold bottle of Heniken over to me, then headed to the other end of the bar to help a customer down there.

Despite the hot man in front of me, my thoughts wandered back to Bowen. He must have a first name, I mused, while taking a long pull on the beer but I could work with calling him Mr. Bowen.

Another long gulp or two and I was giggling to myself and having a fantasy about working under Mr. Bowen, literally. He seemed like he could be an asshole, but you didn't end up behind a desk like his without knowing how to be in control.

Catching me grinning to myself, the bartender strolled back over and stroked a hand over my cheek. Fuck, he was cute! We made some small talk about the interview, which led him to reach out and pull me in for a fast kiss. I said he was a cute bartender, not a good bartender!

Finishing the beer and thanking him for the lead, I dropped him a wink, then slid off the stool and headed out into the afternoon. I had no more than gotten to the doorway when my phone rang. It was the secretary from Bowen's office, ice queen Claire.

I could give you the particulars but the bottom line is that I was offered the job. Hired. I was told I was starting immediately.

Wow!

That was a fast decision!

Suspicious?

Me?

No.

And I didn't care that there would be a pack of peroxide blonds roaming the streets still looking for work Monday.

Katie Scarlett O'Hara like, I mentally shook my fist at the sky and vowed to never go hungry again.

TWO

It was Friday night, the clubs were hopping and I was again in the ranks of the employed! Within seconds I was on every social networking site I belonged to sharing my news with friends, enemies and every casual trick and bar buddy I had in my contact file before I began drinking my way through the bars of Portland. The only place I did not share my joy was the apartment I lived in and hoped to not live in much longer. Things were finally looking up and I didn't want to bring in any darkness, so let Frick and Frack live without the happy news. Removing my tie, I rolled it up and stuck it in my pocket as I continued on until I was drunk enough to be ready to get my dance on, shaking what certainly would have been my money maker again in a very short time had this job not come through.

There aren't many dance clubs in our little jewel of a city on the Willamette River, so when I say I ended up in the largest of them, don't be too impressed. It is a good club, don't get me wrong, and a fun club. But more importantly, it is OUR club and therefore can be all but incestuous, as you see the same faces over and over. Our inbreeding was kept at bay by a decent enough mix of guys who were willing to troll up and down the long narrow ribbon of asphalt known that stretched from being the King George Highway in Vancouver, British Columbia and on into the states where it became Interstate 5, knifing through the center of Seattle and weaving on down to Portland. Some weekends the roadway was thick with gay club fun seekers passing each other in city trades from Van to Seattle and back down to PDX, our own little short hand for our beautiful city.

Word (via ME) had even gotten to the bartender at the dance club, who was NOT a fan of Wyatt Taylor, that I was again employed, so he promptly suggested with a snarl I now PAY UP on some long overdue tabs I had run up over the last few months, now that I was back in coin of the realm. Well, soon to BE back in realm coin.

Slamming the drink he had (sloppily!) scooted over to me, I saluted him with two fingers thrown from my forehead, then flipped him off as soon as he turned back to the register and hustled my way out onto the dance floor where I was greeted like a conquering hero! My friends! Family! (well, bar family), Tricks! Enemies and frenemies bunched up against me as a Kelly Clarkson remix blasted, all of us moving up and down like we were in a giant bouncy house; arms akimbo above our heads. Alvin Ailey eat your heart out 'cause you got nothin' on a buncha drinking gays on a dance floor on a Saturday night! Well, guess you and Mark Morris DO know a thing or twenty about bein' gay on a Friday night.

By then the drinks are flowing as freely as the cold Willamette, grinding is happening all over the place. Some cute kid from Salem is wearing my jacket. Well, he had no shirt and we were making out and one thing led to another….my shirt was open to my belly button, every time I moved you could catch a glimpse of that sexy little dent in my stomach if you were looking. And guys were looking. I wasn't that far away from still being porn cut so like to show those abs, and the rest of the package is pretty easy on the eye, if I say so myself.

And I do….

When you couple that with the fact that due to being part of a couple, then breaking up and being broke, I had been a financial recluse since I didn't have the funds to pay for my share of rounds, so yeah, I'm payin' it up drink wise along with some party favors, so I had hit the cash machine hard, pulling out most of the rest of the little bit of security I had left and was letting the good times roll! Suppliers had found me, treats were paid back and distributed – I was by then a sexy, rumpled (for reals by then, not the mental rumple of the office earlier), paying-my-own-way kind of mess, but no one cared because I was young and cute and more importantly spending as if I had it.

I had no idea what time it was, and like casinos and cathedrals, gay bars are notorious for not showing clocks. I stumbled out of the men's room, snorting like I had pneumonia and happy as a kid at Disney when I ran into a tall, willowy blond who looked like Lucifer seconds before he was banished from heaven. He met my energetic grind against his hips match for match, then leaned down and we made out for a few minutes; his soft, sexy full lips had been plumped with something that got me very excited. I was all for dropping my pants and doing it right there (okay, okay; things like that HAD happened in that bar....), but I was grabbed and drug back onto the dance floor by the guy I had been dancing and making out with before the bathroom break. Hand holding my arm firmly, I was worked back into the crowd and greedily (hey it had been a slow spell for me) cranked my head back to stare through the writhing bodies to see if the sexy blond was even looking at me as I buttoned my shirt, adjusted my belt and peeled the cute kid from Salem out of my now sweat/beer/cigarette smoke (trips had been made outside....) and several other not so readily identifiable smells smelling jacket. In my primordial haze I realized I was pretty wasted and only had about forty-eightish or so hours to SOBER up and become employed.

I made minimal good nights as I worked my way off the dance floor and out of the party, which would rage on for hours (or days) without me. My largess would be missed, but not me, but that was the way my bar crew rolled and I knew that going in so was not upset that no one followed me home or tried to get me to stay. We were used to each other's vanish and appear routines.

I don't remember the rest of the night and did wake alone. Which normally would be a bad thing in my world but I did have the company of a roaring hangover. Given how awful I felt, I was happy not to go through the morning angst of dealing with a stranger. Nothing about me did not hurt; hair, teeth and tongue ached, so being alone was a good thing. My full bladder, however, had my undivided attention, so I got up to attend that, and stopping at the kitchen sink on the way back from the bathroom, I dropped my head under the faucet and gulped as much cold water as I could hold. Then with herky jerky steps, I made it back to my small bedroom.

I'd finally lost the war and given THEM the BIG bedroom, and settled back down after re-fluffing the pillows.

A little more comfortable, I closed my eyes and was on the verge of dropping off again when my phone started blowing up.

I did not want to answer, but I did. It might have been the cute guy from Salem, or another of the I-5 gang I had ground on and exchanged numbers with – a cute Mountie from Vancouver – or one of my rather many creditors, or my mother who would, like the creditors, just keep calling until she got ME rather than use voice mail.

So I manned up and grabbed the phone, but it was none of them. Despite the fact that I had been unemployed for a long time, I thought I had days rather than hours to get myself back to the land of the living and cleaned up enough to report back to the swank office, so was more surprised than I probably should have been when I recognized the voice on the other end of the line as that of Claire (sounding more like the *Elephant Walk* Elizabeth Taylor than the *Who's Afraid of Virginia Woolf* Elizabeth Taylor), my new buddy from the front office of Bowen Industries.

Bicycle horns, Meat packing documentaries? T shirt collars? I should have perhaps done a little more Google homework and a little less drinking.

"'Lo," I managed to mutter with as little commitment and conviction as possible.

"Mr. Bowen wants you at Rose Bud by eight thirty."

The low throaty voice speaking to me from the Bowen Industries reception room might as well have been using Mandarin to communicate. What the fudge was a Rose Bud?

"Rose what?"

"Welcome to Bowen. Be in front of your building at eight. Sharp."

The line went dead before I could ask anything else.

"You are on call twenty-four hours a day, seven days a week."

Bowen's line from the interview rang through my head like a gunshot. With a groan I rolled out of bed and stumbled back to the bathroom where the toilet had just finished running. It was seven forty five and I had rolled into bed at about six. Fucker was testing me from the start, so I made a vow to be ready.

Mr. Bowen (chicken farms? Lanyard weaving? Managing the trust fund of a cobblers union? What DID they do?) did not, whatever the profit making venture of the business, skimp on the car he sent. When I stumbled outside ten minutes later, a black executive town car sat curbside by the hovel we lived in. The driver might just as well have been carved out of stone, or perhaps Bowen hired only the deaf to drive.   Or had their tongues been ripped out? Everything from my greeting ("Hey!" said with as much enthusiasm as I could muster) to my request that we stop at McDonalds (grease and caffeine could not hurt how I felt or what I was about to get into) were ignored.

Silently, save for the growl in my stomach, we rolled though the Saturday morning bustle of the city. I was usually not up until much later so had no idea of what the world was up to at that hour, and it seemed to be pretty much everything. Riding bikes, walking dogs, pushing children in strollers. The people, even their dogs, all looked awake, alert and like they were enjoying being out that early when they could just have easily been sleeping in.

The car passed through the city streets, turning to nose up onto one of the hillsides the city is built on. The higher you went on this particular hill, the more power, money and prestige you held in the Rose city. The silent driver didn't stop until we were at the very tippy top, finally turning off onto a narrow, unmarked lane that seemed to be nothing but a set of ruts at first. A few yards in, untrimmed tree branches scraping the car lightly, the road widened, smoothed out and turned to pavement as the ground around us became more manicured. So groomed in fact it looked like a troop of Korean nail salon workers had been brought in and were trimming, hacking, pruning and shaping each branch, shrub and tree on the park like grounds. At a small gate house a guard nodded as we drove past, a small gate bar lifting. It did not look strong enough to hold back a bicycle let alone a car, but there was an implication that you better have proper authorization or a tank to continue on that roadway.

We ground to a halt in front of a house. A big house. A house like you would see on a movie set or an estate in the French countryside. A house that would make Donald Trump say, "Wow." The place was not small in other words. The driver did not make a move to get out and open the door for me (not that I expected him to), so I said thanks and pushed my way out.

I was about to knock on the huge doors, half expecting the gate guard from wall around the Emerald City in the *Wizard of Oz* to pop out of a porthole in the door before the massive piece of wood work slowly swung open.

"Hi, I'm James," a cute moon faced young man said from the other side of the gap between the door and house.

The keeper of this kingdom was clearly in command. Adjusting his glasses, James switched out the notebooks he held to his other arm and extended a hand. The voice on the other end of the line that morning had not told me what to wear, so I had settled on a high end pair of A/X jeans "borrowed" from the ex's laundry basket (okay, there were some perks to living with not me but two guys who wore about the same size as me, their Romeo and Romeo style love that would not be denied aside) paired with a white button down shirt. James was wearing jeans and a dark polo shirt and a rather haughty attitude, but I was the newbie in this.

"I'm the property manager and you are here to get an overview and inventory. I handle most everything here, but there might be times when you are needed to help out with an event or entertaining, so you need to know how Rose Bud operates, so let's get started."

While we had not been formally introduced, I took it that the house was named Rose Bud.

Sigh. What the fudge HAD I gotten into?

James was the kind of gay, it turned out, who could be seen from space. Once the ice thawed between us, he wore that pull over as if it were made of chiffon and despite the loafers on his feet, I knew in his mind he was in five inch come get me pumps. My kind of gay, in other words. Some guys only want their gays to be straight acting, but I want mine as out as I am and James fit that bill to the hilt.

And get started we did.

Oof.

Rose Bud, one of several homes on the Bowen property that had a name and a manager, had been built by one of Bowen's robber-baron city founding relatives who had stripped the hillsides and brought in rails and industry. But those are necessary in the development of any city, so who am I to judge merit or worth? The senior Bowens had lived in Rose Bud for generations. After they were gone, William Bowen Jr., my new employer at Bowen Industries, had moved into the largest piece of housing real estate. I wondered if the family actually wore rank indicators on their clothing.

"This is the suite for you when you are needed to stay over," the houseman said while opening dresser drawers followed by opening a walk-in closet where a row of black, dark blue and grey suits hung neatly. Giving me the now nearly expected "Bowen Glance" up and down, James said that I might need some tailoring, but I tried on one of the jackets at his request and found it to be a perfect fit.

"Mr. Bowen is particular about the way assistants look. He does have some material to work with in you," he muttered to himself while closing the closet door. Pausing, the cute house manager gave me a quizzical look like he was trying to recognize me. I hoped it was not for the porn work. "I'll send some of these over to your home." He finished, the moment of the uncomfortable look passing quietly.

Well. The clothes were in place, so of course I started a Me-as-Lord-of-the-manner fantasy. I would stun William Bowen with my work and soon he would start making eyes at me which would lead to a love of the ages of my own and me soon doing charity work next to the other wives of Portland's movers and shakers. And rubbing my fab new life in the faces of the ex's as often as possible.

James, I was soon to learn, was not only laser focused on the details of running Rose Bud (all toilet tissue must be folded to a point, and there were a lotta johns in that place....) and the road show of the house did not stop until just after one thirty PM when we ended up in the kitchen. A very serious chef in very serious chef drag moved around the huge, light filled room. James led us to an eating nook set for two. Sliding in, he motioned that I should have a seat as well.

As soon as we were settled, the chef brought over salad plates. I could have fallen asleep had I not been so hungry right then, the numbers of Rose Bud dancing in my head like sheep over a fence. The thread count of each sheet, how many floral arrangements for daily and seasonal use, number of deliveries per day, where they were made – there was a process! I was sweating like I had been wearing a wool sweater in a sauna and James knew it. His grin became mischievous.

"Jean, this is Wyatt, the new assistant." The chef, not missing a beat, gave me the up and down, then turned back toward the massive stove. He was hot but not exactly the chatty type. I'd worry about becoming HIS bestie later.

"Thoughts so far," James said as we started eating. I wasn't about to open up to this guy until I knew him a little better though. He'd been on this ship awhile and knew where the life rafts were.

"Lotta moving parts here," I said, after swallowing a mouthful of salad greens so light they may as well have been made from marshmallows and covered in a dressing I could have drunk like wine. "Does everyone working on the grounds work for Bowen or are they outsourced?" I asked, meaning does he use prisoners as help? Every corner we had turned seemed to have another group of attractive guys doing repair work or cleaning. And there were a lot of corners we turned in the last few hours.

James smiled while Jean came over and removed the salad plates. I was still in mid bite but the surly cook pulled the plate away before I could protest. My gut was still growling and I would have started gnawing on the shrubs had we not stopped for lunch when we did. Individual soufflé cups filled with a perfectly tan, perfectly risen something that smelled the way I imagine heaven or parts of Brad Pitt to smell were dropped in front of us. I was glad to be still holding onto my fork.

"Ah, you noticed the Bowen Lost Boys," James grinned as he shoved a bite of food into his mouth. He had dropped his salad fork and picked up the next one in on the setting. Playing follow the leader, I regained my composure and did the same. I had gotten the job but now needed to keep it and assumed using the correct utensil would point me in that direction.

I had a dozen immediate questions about the lost boys but lunch took a turn when a new player came into the scene.

THREE

The young man who came into the kitchen was tall, which was only part of the reason I recognized him right away. The other reason was that only a few hours earlier I had been grinding on him like he was an herb under the pestle of me. I vaguely remembered him as the kid I'd run into coming out of the men's room in the club. We didn't have sex or anything, but there had been some serious heavy petting going on. He was now wearing two hundred dollar sunglasses and a bathing suit not much bigger than a thong; his feet were jammed into a pair of distressed leather bronze Dolce and Gabbana boots. Without a glance at us he went to the refrigerator and pulled it open, hooking out a can of diet coke. Snapping the top open, the willowy blond lifted it and chugged about half the contents as he sauntered to the table and dug a finger into the soufflé in front of James. Jamming the portion into his mouth, he slowly and seductively pulled the long digit from his mouth.

"You the new guy?"

"Wyatt, this is Colton," James said, in a neutral tone that dripped with venom.

The tall blond took another dig into the soufflé and nearly gave me a smile before sweeping through a set of French doors leading to the sparking pool like Loretta Young. He probably had an outfit for every mood and occasion. This morning the young man of the house wore an ensemble that marked his mood as feeling like a storm trooper/slut.

When I had money, back in the days of porn and roses, I enjoyed shopping too. I still had a few high end Armani and Ben Sherman pieces left, after having sold most of the good stuff to friends who had admired them, for pennies on the dollar. I now got new stuff from thrift shops or by the pound at warehouse stores.

"The current lead in the Lost Boys production here on the plantation," James said, with a dead on southern drawl. He had been nothing but facts and figures all morning and suddenly pulls this big wad of personality out of his purse, so I pounced on the moment like a lion on a zebra. Well, the gay lion on the gay zebra. The bite of soufflé melting in my mouth, I still managed to smile back at his Foghorn Leghorn impression. It was good and more importantly I wanted him on my side.

"Know him?"

"Only if we are going off line. Talk," I said as I swallowed.

A grin wide as a grand piano keyboard crossed the houseman's face.

"Lost Boy? Not really," I said as casually as I could, while cramming more of the melt-in-your-mouth food between my lips like it was going to be taken from me. Well, the salad had set a certain precedent and I was taking no chances. "We just danced a little."

"That's good because he is the current Mr. Bowen. And I have it on good authority he went down on everything but the *Titanic* before landing our Billy. Bring your tea and let's walk while your food settles. You wanna know about Bowen and I wanna know the latest on our Colton." James rose as he spoke.

I guess the starving Cocker Spaniel look I gave him let the property manager know I wanted to finish my lunch and perhaps raid the pantry followed by a trip to Food Giant for some snacks. I was probably still more drunk than hung over and had reached the EAT portion of the program. And since I hadn't had much access to finding food recently, I was like a bear getting ready for hibernation just in case this didn't work out so well.

"Hungry much?" James said, smile back in place as I scooped out another lighter than air bite and brought it to my lips. How could a cook so sour and mean make food so good? I didn't care, Dick Cheney could have been over by the stove and I would have gone all, "More please, Sir?" on his ass. He pushed his finger gorged food over to me with a grin.

"Gotta watch my boyish figure, anyway."

"I bet you gotta lot of other guys watching it for you," I snarked, while snatching at the offered dish. My stomach was roiling but I was storing up like a camel now that I sensed a connection with James. I was about to scrape the ramekin the soufflé was served in when stoic Jean stomped to the table and swept it clean of dishes, utensils – well everything but our glasses of iced tea.

"What am I into here, really?" I finally asked when we were out of earshot of the pool, where Colton had settled into a lounge chair and was sipping his soda while leafing through a very glossy magazine which had far more photographs than print.

"Bowen can trace his family back to France from about the thirteen hundreds. They wouldn't have been caught dead on the *Mayflower* or any other of those group transports. They brought their own ship, then proceeded to buy their way across the country. The Bowens only stopped here because they ran outa land to purchase. I mean you can literally follow the ancestors' route in land holdings because they haven't sold squat since they got here." While he walked, I had been following puppy-like behind him up a long low grade. Stepping aside he swept out an arm and I saw a view like an oil painting behind him.

I gasped. The view was stunning.

"Nice real estate, huh?"

"Yyeah….," I managed to sigh while having a fantasy that Bowen would fall in love with me and that I would change my name to his and forget those that had brung me to the dance down in the lower part of the state.

Turning, James nodded toward the house.

"John Jacob Astor built Fort Astoria in 1811. The Bowens built this house," again he nodded toward Rose Bud, "in 1856. You can see where a sense of entitlement comes from."

"Hey, I'm generational Oregon, too," I protested.

"Yeah, but did your family write the history books?" James sat down and nodded that I should park on the manicured grass next to him. "The house was last done over by Sister Parish and could still be photographed for *AD* tomorrow. Well, once I put fresh flowers in. THAT is how big the money here is, which pretty much sums it up. Old money works differently than new and like most old money families, one of them being openly gay did not fit into the Bowen mold. You can be missing part of an arm, have the mental capacity of a child; the family tree was littered with drunks and abusers. Wasn't a man in the clan who didn't keep a mistress and went through rental women like they were water. But being out and proud was literally the forbidden fruit." James glanced over at me with a sigh while I took another sip of tea.

"Mamma was a southern belle who never transplanted to the north, so she drank. Pappa Bowen toed the family line because that was all he knew. They tried to straighten Billy out but no one harnesses him so he acted out, brought home the baddest of the bad boys. I've been here a long time and trust me, Colton is NOT the worst of the bad lot Portland has had to offer."

I took a sip of tea as my new friend went on.

"Billy is the end of the family line and they knew it when they died; they bribed him, offered to pay him to marry or at least have a kid, but he held firm. And he won. All of this is his." James spread his arms to indicate the national park-like setting we were in; correction, that PRIVATE national park with a mansion in the middle of it we were in.

Before James could continue, his phone rang and he jumped up as if he had a spring in his ass, motioning me to follow him. Back at the house, the small phone sill slammed against his ear, James had me follow him into the house and handed me a manila envelope while still talking. Using a shooing motion, he brushed me out the back door where I was met by a grounds man who began instructing me on how to care for the pool and ponds and, well, grounds in general.

And that was the last I saw of James for a while. I later learned from James that the workers on Plantation Bowen (Rose Bud and grounds), those *Lost Boys*, were various tricks, their buddies pals from over the years Bowen had hired on and allowed James to wrangle as the upkeep on the massive place. A win-win of community service of sorts as it kept them employed and off the streets from terrorizing citizens at large with their outlandish costumes, make-up and vicious tongues. For the most part good kids put to hard labor but well cared for by the firm. Bowen was very waste not, want not in other words and recycling even his guys once he was done with them.

Sunday was spent nursing another hangover, the one I had picked up from going out Saturday night and partying almost as hard as I had on Friday night. I wasn't used to this work thing. I had stuffed the manila envelope James had given to me into a carry satchel, planning to go over it on my way to the office on Monday.

However, Monday morning I found myself on a different agenda. I arrived at Bowen an hour ahead of my scheduled time for work at nine AM., pacing in front the massive downtown building that had been a cornerstone of the city since it had been a tiny trading post back in the eighteen something's. Farm kids, in addition to learning about cows and sex and eggs and all THAT stuff learn about being early for everything no matter how tired or, well let's face it, hung over I was.

Luckily, I moved in fifteen minutes early, hoping to schmooze Claire into at least a semblance of friendship. She was not behind the desk. I was about to call out "Hellooo..." when she appeared behind me. I jumped three feet into the air (it seemed) but my fall was cushioned by the knee deep cashmere carpet covering the floor.

"Why are you here?" It was a demand, not a question.

"I was hired here," I started, only to be cut off. That happened a lot to the low guy on the totem around here it seemed.

"You were hired to be where Mr. Bowen is," Claire barked as she slid in behind the huge command central-like desk, slamming down into her space age design chair that probably cost more than the annual salary I had been promised. She reattached herself to a headset, then turned and stared at me like I were criminally insane before continuing.

"If you had read the material you OBVIOUSLY did not read you would know that you should be at the airport, where Mr. Bowen is. Sending the new one down, see if you can get him to the airport in time." She went on briskly. I started to say something (stupid) but she just pointed toward the bank of elevators without turning around. How could I get on her good side? Chocolates? Flowers? Find her house and paint her garage.

The silent driver was waiting for me in the garage and broke a sound barrier or two getting me to a private runway just beyond the city limits I would never have found with a GPS and a Girl Scout guide.

Mounting the small staircase I jumped into the little plane and buckled myself into one of the free seven seats. William Bowen, my ruggedly hot employer, was already strapped into the eighth seat.

"Good Morning!" I called out with a cheer I did not feel. I was hardly familiar with how much to pay per ride on the Portland Public transit bus system and now here I was strapped into the seat of a *private* jet for my first plane ride.

Turning, Mr. Bowen gave me a glare and I realized he was talking into a Bluetooth device. I was forming something more (stupid) to say when a pilot who looked like he was scheduled for a photo shoot with *Playgirl* later in the day came into the cabin. Wordlessly, he and Mr. Bowen gave each other a thumbs up and Captain Hotness disappeared back into the cockpit. The door was latched closed by someone and before I could turn to see who we were first doing a taxi then had swooshed down the runway and were in the air.

Almost, sadly, before I could keep from squealing like a puppy being held too tight by a three year old, I yelped. I tried to keep the noise in, I really did, but the body is an amazing thing and stuff happens. Toldja I'd never been on a plane. A startled Mr. Bowen swung around in his seat, giving me a look of confusion.

"Alright?"

I nodded yes while holding onto the armrest like a cartoon cat. The look on my face (and roundness of my eyes) must have told him a different story because he reached down to the side of his seat and unlatched it, allowing it to swing around so that we were nearly face to face. His perfectly pressed shirt and tie made me even more nervous for some reason.

"Thought this might give us a chance to talk. We are going to San Diego for a meeting, then back here for a late afternoon meeting. You have the agenda for the rest of the week, right?"

I could only nod; the g force not only held me back into the seat but seemed to have frozen my tongue. I felt like we were on the edge of space. *"One small step for man...,"* rang through my head as I tried to focus on Bowen, sexy as he was, especially this close, but even that couldn't distract me from being hurled through space. If this rocket from hell ever landed, I'd just stay wherever we touched down, I was deciding. There were beaches in San Diego, right? I'd live on one of them. I'd swim instead of bathe, learn to catch fish and cook them over open fire. Perhaps someday I'd again find another job and start anew. Bonus! The Bobbsey twins wouldn't be in my living space fondling each other and I'd really not been with Bowen Industries long enough for them to give me a bad reference. That's me, King of turning things around and finding silver linings!

"Charles, bring some water!" Bowen suddenly yelped as I tried to speak and unclench my fingers from the arm rest but found myself frozen. Mr. Bowen stared at me until the (sexy! blond!) flight attendant arrived with a bottle of water. Letting Charles attend me, Bowen gave me a look of disgust and turned his chair back around, the sound of the lock clicking in place like a reproach. Charles gave me the smile of another indentured servant who really can't help the situation and I made a mental note to get his story from James.

Gratefully accepting the water, I finally twisted my head slightly enough to look out of the small window, realizing the particulars of the job had perhaps purposely not been discussed. Particulars like, "Have you ever flown at the speed of light?" or "Can you pH balance a hot tub and arrange dinner for fifteen on an hour's notice." It was making sense to me that the weekend training at Rose Bud and this first day of the new job were tests. Which was good enough reason, along with getting to wear those nifty suits and enjoying FOOD again, not to quit or ask that we land that little George Jetson size vehicle on the freeway RIGHT THEN because I was feeling queasy.

Actually, I would have to go some distance back UP to just feel queasy.

Taking a few sips of water, I concentrated as hard as I could on controlling the fluttering in my stomach. No butterflies for this kid, I had some kinda dinosaur stomping around down there in my gut. I could feel rings of sweat circling out down under my arms despite the deodorant I had slathered on not all that long ago. I hoped the circles of fear and flop sweat that had formed in the suit wouldn't ruin it because if I hocked everything I owned I'd still not be able to come up with enough to pay for it.

Mr. Bowen had gone back to muttering to himself in the next seat over. I was certain he was on the phone to his office, instructing Claire to get another troop of blond Scandinavians back for another round of interviews. I was making an impression, not a good one just a big one.

Like all good times, this one came to an end, the plane coming in for a fast, smooth landing while my stomach lurched like it was on full boil.

"Just follow me and observe," Mr. Bowen said as we entered stepped off an elevator in a downtown high rise, "for God's sake go in the restroom and freshen up though!" he finished briskly but not unkindly. The warm seaside city air had hit me in the face like a wet sock full of cotton balls. Mr. Bowen was used to climate changes but you might as well have dropped me in the middle of the arctic. A slight shudder (and a suppressed urge to whimper) were added to my little display of bodily functions and while I was wearing a very expensive suit, I now looked like I had just come out of that big club of ours at day break-between the lurching, shuddering and beaded sweat on my forehead.

Jerking his head to the left, I peeled off and went into a beautifully appointed men's room, complete with sofa and real hand towels. I was sizing it up as a potential living space when I caught sight of myself in the (huge!) plate glass mirror and saw why Mr. Bowen wanted me to clean up. I was ghost white, deep circles had set in under my eyes and the glassy sheen of sweat on my skin made me look like a corpse.

I was a hot mess, in other words.

I cleaned myself up as quickly as I could, splashing cold water on my face, then dragging my fingers through my hair and straightening my tie. Not great but decidedly better, I thought, as I smacked my cheeks a few times, then went back into the reception area. The (hot!) young man behind the reception desk did a double take, then cracked a half grin of recognition. The porn had made it to San Diego ahead of me.

Bowen, not used to waiting I was certain, bolted through a massive doorway next to the desk. I had to ask James about that door situation, this one was even more impressive than the one to Bowen's office. Were castles being dismantled and sold for profit? I guess doors were a status symbol in the corporate world.

"Billy Bowen!" a short man with a frizz of grey hair yelped from behind a massive desk, a red Ralph Lauren polo stretched over a swag of gut. The mostly bald top of his head reflected the bright sunshine streaming in through the floor to ceiling windows as he grabbed Mr. Bowen's hand and pumped it while ignoring him completely as he locked his eyes on me like I was made of chocolate ice cream.

"Lewis Frazier!" he continued, eyes never leaving mine as he dropped Bowen's hand and thrust his wide palm over to me. It felt like a leech as it grabbed me; his paw was moist, the dampness actually seemed to seal our skin together. I didn't understand why Bowen had me go freshen up, as Mr. Frazier had mentally stripped me naked and tossed me on top of the "in" box on his desk or filed me under "things to do."

Trying to turn a grimace into a grin, I pulled my hand away and fell back into a chair at the back of the room as the two men sat and started talking. Mr. Bowen ignored the fact that at every other word Mr. Frazier glanced at me. I had no idea what the meeting was about, but busied myself trying to take notes of a sort and ended up instead making a column of numbers to use my tiny bit of UNemployment on in the next few weeks, because if getting sick on the plane, wrinkling the beautiful suit I was wearing, and not winking back at the man behind the desk who was flapping his right eye up and down at me like it had tourettes didn't get me fired, nothing would.

"Let's have lunch over at the yacht club," Lew leered, "I'll show you where I moor my dinghy!"

The thought of a paycheck in my account by the middle of the next week kept me in my chair, rather than jumping up with a scream and running out past the hot receptionist.

"Sorry Lew, gotta get back." Mr. Bowen smiled, saving the day as the cute guy from the front came through the doorway pushing a cart with a coffee service and sandwiches or pastry or blood sausage because we were breaking something with Lew Frazier, by golly, whether Bowen wanted it or not.

Business discussed (whatever it had been), Frazier now busied himself handing Mr. Bowen a cup of coffee and a plate with something baked or broiled or fried on it. Turning, he shoved a tall glass of orange juice into my hand.

Nervously and to be polite, I took a gulp, not noticing at first that about half of the glass had spilled over onto my shirt; the juice staining down over my shirt, tie, and onto the pants of the beautiful suit. Jumping up like I was on fire, I grabbed a handful of napkins from the service cart, cutting my eyes over to see Lew Frazier grinning like he'd won the lottery at seeing my misfortune.

"Oh, accidents happen, calm down!" he said, as if the whole thing had been planned. "Go into my washrooms; in fact, there are some sweats and shoes in there – just leave the suit and wear them. I'll have your clothes cleaned and get them back to you."

I looked at Mr. Bowen, who to his credit seemed to be genuinely embarrassed for me. If this didn't get me a bus ticket over to the beach instead of a plane ride home, nothing would.

Mr. Frazier's bathroom was big, bigger than the bathroom in the reception area, complete with a floor to ceiling mirror, full shower/steam room combo. It was like a spa in there and I immediately changed my assessment of living spaces as this area was bigger than my entire apartment! Peeling out of the juice sticky clothes, I found a hanger in a small closet. Yup, a closet! In a bathroom! Carefully hanging up the pieces of the suit, I stepped into the shower and cleaned up, luxuriating in the heat and steam, then hooking a towel as thick and fluffy as a sheep off the top of a stack in a basket on the floor. I changed into a pair of clean sweats that were suspiciously small for the rotund frame of Lew Frazier, then put on the socks and training shoes that felt like they had been custom made for my feet. Giving another quick drag of my fingers through my hair, I went back into the office where the two men were talking in low voices.

"See! Nothing to get upset over!" Mr. Frazier grinned, holding his hands out toward me. I thanked him and we were finally out of the uncomfortable meeting.

"I am so sorry, Mr. Bowen. I..." Raising his hand, he cut me off.

"Work on it," was all he said tersely.

We were soon back in the Rose city and I was excused from the afternoon meeting, not because I was again queasy on the flight home, but because I needed to meet the fun folks from Human Resources who, after a mountain of their paperwork, sent me downtown to a doctor's office where I was poked, prodded, scraped and asked to pee in a cup. Hair was plucked from my scalp and eye lashes – there was not a heck of a lot I was not asked to excrete for testing and examination. I was told due to insurance criteria I would have to report for blood testing every three months. From there I went on to the tailor for measurements, a very nice Italian man who ran a tape over every inch of my body and told me the suits I had been given would be custom fit to meet the Bowen corporate image. I was finally sent to a photography studio where I was photographed in briefs to suit and casual wear. Odd? Yeah, but they were even *dressing* me you have to understand, so I would not have questioned it had they asked me to go out and feed the company zebra and rhino. I would have just asked the way to the zebra and rhino food room.

The next morning Claire gave me a tour of the upper floor offices we were in, and finally opened the door to the small suite (yup, I said suite – office with closet and attached ¾ bath – bet Bowen had a tub in his....) where I would work. And the gym downstairs, complete with FULL size pool, a private locker assigned to me (I could use the facilities 24/7), and up to the private rooftop restaurant where I was to just SIGN for meals.

I had come home.

FOUR

I made it through the first week (the tests had amazingly come back negative!) and I had not been fired. While I started to get comfortable on the plane rides, I was again clumsy in Salt Lake City (coffee in my crotch, changing in another perfect private bathroom), Billings (Milk), Chicago (iced tea). I had never been so damp until I started to travel with Bowen! But all of the corporate executives and company owners didn't seem to mind. I was blotted, swiped and wiped with towels in every office that had a jovial, squatish guy behind a desk when we entered and ended with me in their bathroom. They all ate me with their eyes, although there were photos on every desk of the men with women and children I assumed to be wives and offspring. I was learning to take notes, Bowen began coaching me on how to take the kind of notes he wanted in our meetings and while I still hadn't figured out quite where I fit into the picture of what went on at Bowen industries, I knew I was proving myself to Bowen even if the suits

I had been gifted to wear were being cleaned like they were costumes in a play.

I also began to take longer showers since no one seemed to mind, even jacking off a few times when the spirit (and my hormones) moved me. The suits would end up back at Bowen and the sweats, gym suits, track wear (sometimes complete with underwear and jocks the men insisted I change into) were shipped back to the men by some mailroom gnome at Bowen. I'd strip out of them, put 'em in a bag and hand 'em over to Claire.

Two months had passed since I had been hired and I was happily settling into a new life. I was, in fact, away so often that when the Gabor boys (well they were dyed blond and ageing) asked if I was interested in saving even more money by all of us continuing to live in the same apartment when the time came to renew the lease, I said sure.

My office in Bowen tower was as good as a Mercedes when it came to pick-ups, anyway. I never even needed to take dates back to the apartment. While I cop to being decent on the eye, I always knew I could seal the deal by casually needing to "swing by the office" late at night to "pick something up" when I had a guy I wanted to nail. Between the private (3/4 remember) bath, view of the city at night, intercom (which still made me jump like the border patrol wanted to see my green card when Claire or

Bowen buzzed it) and flat screen mounted on the wall, I was all but assured a romp on the (leather!) sofa with no one the wiser that I had been in after hours.

"Mr. Bowen is heading to the airport. You are going to Las Vegas for a casual weekend with clients." Claire announced one Friday afternoon. I was used to travel with no notice by then and kept a suitcase packed with essentials. What I didn't take with me could always be found at the hotel we were at. The best part of that was that it went right onto the Bowen account!

I also had come to really love those suits hanging like meeting armor in a neat row in that closet and was even happier that all of the spillage had not ruined any of them. The tailor had fit them to my body so that every crease fell perfectly and my crotch had, frankly, never been better showcased. Bowen didn't seem to notice, but every client sure did. Most of them met me with a long stare below the waist before moving up to my (ok, ok SPARKLING) eyes. But I had other great clothes from Bowen as well; jeans, (tight!), polos (even tighter!), t shirts (tightest of all!); sweaters, underwear and socks, everything the well dressed assistant to a man like William Bowen would ever need to always look his best.

So I packed up some casual wear and hit the garage where Stony, as I had nicknamed the driver of silence, was waiting. It was mid afternoon and we had about an hour and a half flight, so I happily snapped a Xanax in half and dry swallowed it. The day after that first flight, Claire had appeared at my office door with a bottle of them, saying Mr. Bowen thought it would be a good idea for me to take half of one whenever I flew. I was REALLY starting to look forward to flying just to get one of the pills.

"Hey," Mr. Bowen SPOKE! To ME!

"HEY!" I responded, with probably too much enthusiasm. The flight attendant, Charles, started locking down and we were suddenly in our departure mode, which ended the conversation which really hadn't even begun. I didn't care because my good buddy Xanax was nicely settled into my system by then.

"We're having dinner with a client tonight, who is also an old friend." Mr. Bowen had suddenly turned his chair and clicked it in place in front of me. "You'll like him."

Oh, I guess I forgot to mention I had dry swallowed the second half of that Xanax just before I got out of the car. I'd been doing that for a while, doubling up just before takeoff on the tiny (fast!) jet. Claire kept the bottle full all of the time, so what the heck.

This was turning into an amazing trip; my first time in 'Vegas, mellowed by the pills and nearly more words directed at me from my employer than I'd ever had.

"Sure!" I agreed, feeling my eyes start to flutter. I was warm and oozy at about 30,000 feet.

Las Vegas! Bright, made brighter by the next half a Xanax I had popped about halfway through the flight in the teeny tiny bathroom of the teeny tiny jet. We passed acres of hotel complexes that lined the strip, the sun was setting, but most of what I saw was just those bright, bright lights outside the tinted windows of the town car which stopped, nearly hypnotizing me when the car stopped and my door was opened by the driver, suitcase taken by a bellman. One of the other (many) perks of travel with Bowen was that I didn't have to open a door or lift a thing when we were on the road doing, well, whatever it was we did on the road, aside from me being damp and spilling on myself a lot. Bowen talked, I spilled, but so far the (healthy!) paychecks had rolled in every other week into my account, so I wasn't asking questions. I mean it wasn't like I didn't have the ability to lift stuff. I had full access to the corporate gym, which had the latest of every kind of machine on the market. The perks were piling up and I was taking full advantage, watching both my guns and bank account grow.

"I'll be at my condo. You're here. Be back down at eight to be picked up for dinner."

Usually my directives came from Claire, but Mr. Bowen was telling me this so who was I to question that I had been deposited in front of the *Wynn* complex and then was escorted to a penthouse suite where I found another half a Xanax hanging out in the bottle and washed that lil' fucker down with a big slug of vodka as I stood surveying the golden desert, the lights of the city clustered like a group of birthday candles of it far below me. For a kid from the sticks of Oregon, I was doing ok! And feeling ok! Not wasted (well, two whole Xanax and half a great big vodka, so I was pretty *relaxed*) and on top of my game enough to put a snappy little outfit together and slam the other half of that drink before getting ready to skedaddle (now THERE is an underused word, huh!) downstairs when there was a knock at the door. A hotel attendant was there holding a small silver tray with an envelope addressed to me. Taking it, I thanked him while fishing for some cash. Luckily I had jammed some singles I was going to hit slots with deep into my pocket so I crammed a few into his palm.

Wyatt, I'm not feeling well and would take it as a personal favor if you would go ahead and have dinner with my friend Tom. He will be downstairs in the restaurant at eight-thirty. Just sign for the meal.

Take tomorrow off. The enclosed is a thank you bonus-hit some slots! Wm. Bowen

The note was folded around ten one hundred dollar bills.

Well, who was I not to be up to some free food on top of the cash? I wasn't over the top drunk (yet...), so kept my balance as I sauntered into the bustling restaurant where the hostess led me to a table. Already seated was a handsome if a little overweight – fact not judgment – man, grey at the temple, twinkling eyes. We introduced ourselves and I, naturally, ordered up another drink.

Tom Overbay of Lincoln, Nebraska, my dining companion for the evening, was probably twenty years older than me, but that sexy network of craggy lines around his eyes, his humor and ease at conversation made him seem like a contemporary. I, on the other hand, wasn't much of a character study because I was loopy and getting loopier. Our conversation wandered from his friendship with William Bowen to my family; we briefly discussed astrophysics, whatever the hell that was, and generally became chummier with each course. Several of my courses were liquid but sometimes you need that all booze dinner.

By the end of the meal, Tim and I were fast friends. Had I been a little more restrained, I would have noted the thick gold wedding band sooner, but as it was, I wasn't aware of it until I was sucking on his finger when we were in bed later and I didn't by then care who else he might be connected to.

But we'll get to that....

When Tom asked what I was doing after dinner, it didn't dawn on me that I had been set up on a date with this guy. He produced tickets to a late show, which was good – well there was booze, so you know I was up for it, then when we left the theatre and he asked if there was anything else I wanted to do, I said *"Let's go dancing!"*, which seemed a perfectly reasonable thing to do. Next thing I knew we were in a car, then on the floor of a gay dance bar shaking our groove thangs.

As the night had progressed, Tom had gotten handier and handier, his touches became longer and more lingering, there was a kiss on my neck on the dance floor and you know what, I liked every blessed one of those caresses! It had been a long time since a guy had paid me any attention and I was getting off on it! I had always had my share of men coming on to me, but in the time I was broke and feeling rejected by everyone including my guardian angel, I had forgotten that there was a pretty hot face reflecting back at me in the mirror. Tom might not have been the guy I set my sights on back in Portland, but I'd learned from that ex and bestie that pretty doesn't mean loyal in the race of love. Tom's arms around me felt good, strong and warm, and yeah, I was pretty drunk off my ass by then but at least I was feeling safe.

So when he followed me back up to that swank penthouse in the hotel, kissing and nuzzling me the whole way, under the pretense of getting me to bed safely, who was I to argue? It was nice to have someone in control. So when he fell onto the bed with me and we began to make out, it was only natural that we went ahead and had some fun. Frankly, I was proud to show off the effects of my long afternoon workouts at the Bowen gym, workout time built into my schedule and blessed by William Bowen, so what the heck. I'd not had that many dates since the breakup and since Tom was right there and felt so good, I just went with the evening.

From what I can remember, Tom was a careful and considerate lover. After fucking me like I had never been fucked, he held me tight and we drifted off.

I'd like to say drifted off, but I actually just kinda passed out. When I awoke, the room was dark, someone (Tom? Housekeeping? A ghost?) had drawn the blackout shades. Tom wasn't in bed with me, so I thought he was out getting coffee or preparing to shower, so I went back to sleep.

Hours later (hey, I was digging this free time not being leashed to the telephone for the day, a rare treat!) when I woke again, I used a remote on the night table to open the shades, revealing the blinding blue sky outlining the jagged mountains that ring the city in the distance. It was an amazing view, even on a queasy stomach. My cock was hard again; hey, I'm a guy and it was morning, so that was a pretty natural way for me to wake up.

Ignoring my quivering dick, I reached over to grab the remote to see if porn was available. I was in a Penthouse and by golly felt entitled to some.

My fingers instead closed on a sheet of folded paper; a confetti of bills rained onto the rumpled bedclothes as I scanned the words;

Wyatt, I only get out to play once a year and you have given me a memory that will last much longer than that. Do some gambling and have some fun on me. Tom

Five more one hundred dollar bills were scattered around me.

This was curious to say the least. I knew I was playing in the big league by just being at Bowen, but how do you handle THIS? Was I just paid to have sex? Should I tell Mr. B. that his friend and client and I had bumped uglies – for fun AND profit it seemed. A lotta questions for just waking up, and still with a piece that was rarin' to go.

I decided to Scarlett O'Hara again and think of the answers another day. And with that I found the porn (those channels are included with the penthouse….) and after a couple of quick rounds of fun-for-one, I ordered up a huge breakfast from room service.

By the time I did meet back up with Mr. Bowen, he was physically feeling better but I could tell he was upset about something. Could he already know about Tom and me? Luckily Bowen was glued to his tablet the whole flight back so I kept my mouth shut and my eyes glued onto my bag that had fifteen hundred bucks cash American tucked into it that I had not come on the trip with.

Later that night, after I had safely hidden that new found cash in my room, a call came in from Claire that gave me a little insight to Bowen's bad mood. More snappish than usual, she told me that I would be picked up early the next morning. Mr. Bowen had a personal task for me to attend and I would need to be prepped.

The current boyfriend, tall and tiny suited Colton, had been arrested (again) for drunken driving while Bowen and I were in Las Vegas. He had been bailed out and taken back to Rose Bud. I would, per Claire, be given instruction on my part of the issue in the car on the way to the house in the morning. The joy and fun of the weekend drained at the thought of taking on whatever this task was, but having fifteen hundred bucks tax free(!) wasn't much of a retirement, so I sucked it up and turned out the lights.

The morning WAS going to be another day, but perhaps not a fun one, I thought to myself.

Next morning, the silent driver was right on time. I called out a cheery *Good Morning!* while scooping up a packet on the seat. I frequently found stiff, buff colored folders waiting for me when I got in the car; expense reports, inventory lists, Rose Bud dinner guest information, coupons to clip – yes, you read that right – and this time the most interesting bill of lading of all.

"Little help here, dude!" I yelped to James once I had bolted from the car and into the house. It was so early Jean the mean was not even in the kitchen to brew coffee. I'd had to drag the house manager from his suite. "This reads like I'm supposed to FIRE his boyfriend! What the fuck!" I was shaking the folder with a single sheet of printed information in it.

"Calm down," James said with a yawn while sliding a kettle onto a burner on the massive stove. "You aren't firing him. Just removing him from the property and telling him never to come back or have contact with William Bowen or Bowen Industries ever again."

"Why didn't you tell me I might have to do something like this?"

"Frankly, I didn't think you'd last this long."

So helpful, my new bud.

"He's done this before?" I sat down at the kitchen table. Well, fell into a chair.

"Of course. It's how he always does it. He's a bulldog in the boardroom and runs the business like he's its Pope, but he just can't shake this bad taste in men." James was pulling cups and saucers from a cupboard as if we were going to stroll the gardens while discussing spring planting instead of me going upstairs to evict Colton. Bringing a tea canister to the table, he carefully filled two silver strainers with loose leaf and put them into out cups before snagging the gurgling kettle off the flame and filled the cups, then sat down. "Welcome to life in the trenches at Bowen. One lump or two?" He slid a plate with two flakey freshly home baked croissants across the table toward me.

"Vodka. I need vodka," I muttered, as James smiled and eased a cube of sugar into each of our cups.

"Liquor would only give you false confidence. This is Early Grey breakfast; it'll give you just the boost you need to get through this."

I started to lift the cup only to have James smack the side of my hand with a dainty silver tea spoon. It felt like I had been stung by an angry gay bee.

"Let it steep!"

"This is insane," I started to rant, only to have the now famous and should-have-been-expected hand raise happen.

"Not really. See, you have to let the ball sit in the hot water to release the flavor." I let him get that far before cutting him off with a glare. "Oh, you mean the Colton thing. Wasn't it F. Scott Fitzgerald who said, *"The rich are not like you and I."* There was a pause as James lifted the cup and took a sip, then looked at me very seriously. "What did you do this weekend?"

"Went to Las Vegas in a private jet and stayed in a penthouse suite......oh," I said, realizing that while what I had been ordered to do WAS nuts but that I HAD bought into the fun, easy part of the job, and now I was expected to deal with the bitter part. The rich really are NOT like you and I.

"Uh huh," James said after another sip, realizing I was starting to understand. "So have your cuppa and man it up. You gotta evil queen to wake up and evict, but I won't tell if you put pillow over his face. Friends help friends move; real friends help friends move bodies," he said, while lifting the wafer thin bone china cup.

I was liking the snarkly twerp more and more.

After two GREAT notes addressed to me, wrapped around money, no less, I shouldn't have expected my next written material to have been any better. And it wasn't. The folder waiting for me in the car had a note inside signed by William Bowen instructing that I should go to the house named Rose Bud in Portland, Oregon, and evict one Mr. Colton Farmer. Colton was to be escorted from the property with the instruction that he not return; he was to leave with only a set of clothing. His belongings would be shipped to the Windsor hotel in downtown Portland where he would be lodged until the end of the week. After that, he was to have no contact with William Bowen or anyone associated with Bowen Industries, Rose Bud or the properties of Bowen Industries.

Sigh.

"How many times has this happened?"

James held up three fingers. "In the five years I have been here. His second time being outed though. Each one of them thought they were THE one. This one's come closest to getting a ring, but I knew it wouldn't last."

"It doesn't go easy, does it?" I shuddered. Didn't gay men ever break-up in civilized ways? Of course, I thought of Jack and Jill back at the apartment and how I had come roaring in on them mating like the primates they were. Well, I had recently sated some primal urges for cash which kinda made me a whore, but THEY didn't need to know that.

The house manager shook his head "no" to my question, then lifted his tea cup. I clicked mine against his.

"You aren't going to help me, are you?"

A grin spread over his face while he shook his head no slowly. With friends like James, you did not need an enemy.

"If I scream, don't just sit here drinking your tea then. Come upstairs, THEN call 911 once you have pried him off me."

"Pat him down before you put him in the ca-ar....," he trilled, while pulling the plate with the pastry on it toward himself and picking at one as I stood and headed toward the stairs. I knew queens like the one I was about to face. I knew club kids like Colton who hadn't partnered up nearly as well as he had. Once they had a taste of living rent free and access to food (and drugs) on a regular basis, they became wolverine vicious to the core, ready to fight for what they felt was theirs. In this case, it was the volcano hot William Bowen, the $100.000 Porsche Colton had gotten used to driving, and that wardrobe of tiny 'n tight things he had amassed. And I would not necessarily list their importance in his life in that order.

This could be my 'Nam.

The master suite was at the top of the stairs, a set of thick double doors not quite as impressive as those at the Bowen offices, but close. Knocking would have been the polite thing, but I didn't know what state I would find the tall blond in, so I just barged in.

Luckily, he was just asleep and not looped out of his head and covered in go-go boys. Flipping on the lights did not bother him at all; his head was burrowed down under the blankets like he was a gopher.

"Colton, it's Wyatt," *Not a creature was stirring, especially William Bowen's spouse...* "Colton.....," I continued. There was a twitch and his left foot popped from under the thick comforter he was wrapped in. I called his named three more times before he snaked his head from under the bed clothes.

"Get the fuck out or get the fuck in and fuck me, stud," the pale, slender blond said in an even voice.

Unexpected commentary.

"Mr. Bowen wants you out, Colton. For what it's worth, I'm sorry."

"You sure as fuck are," he snarled, head pulling fully out into the light. His blond hair was spiked and shot with silver glitter and he looked like crap warmed over; blood shot eyes, skin pale and drawn.

"If I promise to go easily, will you suck me off first?"

I had no response for that, so just stood quietly as the blond leered.

"Why this time?"

I kept up my silence. I'd learned a thing or three from the driver who had been schlepping me around the last few months.

"The DUI thing," Colton mused, "second or third car I've wrecked, too. THAT really pisses him off."

"Just go, Colton. He's putting you up in a hotel for a week. Let him cool off and call him." Get me, like I wanted him around as a further complication in all our lives. "He's going to send your things."

"What if I call him and tell him you jumped on the bed and took me, pinned me to the mattress and pounded me like flank steak with that big 'ol dick of yours," a grin crossed his face.

The men in this house smirked at the oddest things; James at my predicament of evicting Colton; Colton at the thought of trying to blackmail me into submission. But perhaps it wasn't their fault. It might have been Rose Bud controlling the emotions like in that great Bette Davis movie from the mid 1970's titled *Burnt Offerings*. Miss Davis stars with Oliver Reed, Eileen Heckart, Burgess Merideth and Karen Black. A family becomes caretakers of a big old estate home (similar to Rose Bud, in fact) for a summer season and the house slowly kills them to rejuvenate to its former glory, keeping Karen Black in the attic as a kind of souvenir. Wouldn't surprise me at all if the upper portion of Rose Bud was filled with ageing party boys.

And perhaps Karen Black.

Slipping from under the comforter, Colton stood in front of me wearing nothing but the glitter in his hair and a tiny pair of bikini style underwear so thin I could tell his religion. The blond had what appeared to be a salami size schlong all but falling out of the silky material. Frankly, I could see Bowen's attraction even if he was hot in a *Twilight* vampire kinda way. Bowen did things in a big way (house, jet, office…) so it made sense that the boss would be a size queen on top of everything else.

Following the gaze of my eyes, Colton dropped a hand to his crotch and jiggled the piece. I won't lie. There was a temptation. He had the body of a swimmer and had sculpted his abs into cum gutter sections, as they well should have been given that keeping his body up was his only job.

"C'mon, let's play," he all but purred. I repeat that I DID fall off a turnip truck but not yesterday. Colton knew he had messed up and knew if he could tempt me that it would at the very least muck things up for me. What he didn't know was that I had nearly seen the bottom of life, well, my life at least, and knew that there was nothing good right below that shallow, shallow skim of water that had covered the bottom when I'd walked in on my boyfriend getting plowed by my best friend and was then unemployed and about to be evicted and, oh, any number of jolly things like that. It would take a heck of a lot more than this poor excuse for a seduction to get me to mess this up. I knew what hunger was and I suspected that Colton did too.

But I had a fresher memory of it than he did.

We stood staring at each other for awhile until Colton, with a sigh, started moving around the room gathering up scattered clothing. I let him take his time dressing while I wondered what had happened the LAST time he was Rose Bud banished to make him actually start moving that quickly.

When he had lazily put together a travel ensemble from the wrinkled clothing strewn around the room and had plucked a pair of sunglasses from the dresser, he turned to me while carefully adjusting the expensive shades over his eyes.

"This will blow over and I'll be back and you'll be gone, so don't give him any diseases," he said evenly with a sneer. Turning, I walked out of the room and without prompting him, Colton followed me down the stairs and out the door to the car with the waiting driver in front of the house.

The bad tooth pulled, I went back into the kitchen, stomach churning, to finish my tea only to find that James had gone back to bed.

I sat down and picked up the thin, expensive cup and took a sip. Who knew, Colton might even be right. He had been dismissed as the boss' boyfriend and I had been the one to throw him out; sure, good things could come of that.

Just in case things went wrong, I decided I'd better find out if it was an asp or an adder Elizabeth Taylor used to off herself with in *Cleopatra*. Plan-wise it wasn't up to my usual *Stone Soup* gold standard, but a plan is a plan and that got me through the morning because the whole "remove" Colton portion of my job program had gone just too quietly for my taste. He was not the kind who just turned and followed, so either I was far more intimidating than I ever thought or there was stuff I didn't know.

FIVE

Once in high school I'd gone as far north as Seattle. We saw the Pacific Science center located at the base of the Space Needle, Lake Washington, and the famous Pike Place Farmers Market. I'd made out with a cute buddy of mine named Kerry in the room we shared but he had chickened out to go any farther than some tentative kissing. So far, that trip was the highlight of my travel life and I still thought of it fondly.

Since moving to Portland I had met people from the exotic state of Idaho and the country of Canada as they passed through our peaceful city in search of adventure, and since becoming a regular on the Bowen Industries (cat food? Pearl rings? Skate board trucks?) payroll (which meant I was again a regular at Safeway and Trader Joe's), I had started to travel on the little jet the way I used to ride the number 7 bus. I've told you about San Diego and Las Vegas, but in the time I had been in the position of #1 to William Bowen there had also been trips to

Seattle, Sacramento, Palm Springs, San Francisco and Terra Haute.

I know! But Indiana in the spring was prettier than I would have thought, if flat! And I slept with each of the married guys Mr. Bowen had come to do business with. They would show me around their city after our meetings, take me to dinner where there would be wine and drinks afterward and yeah, pot in a few cases. The next morning the guy would be gone from my hotel room, leaving a nice note and a chunk of "pocket money" in the form of one hundred dollar bills on a table near the bed.

I was popular with the clients!

Mr. Bowen happily signed huge contracts!

And I wore an internal ostrich outfit like it was Gucci! Never questioning any of this!

We would come back to Portland and I would squirrel the money away in my room back at *Heartbreak Hotel*. The "we are SO much in love" Ron and Nancy Reagan like couple I lived with would have sent away for a truck load of mixed Asps and Adders for me if they'd had any idea of the little *Chase* branch I had hidden in a couple of shoe boxes under my bed.

And now here I sat on that zippy little private jet again, my travel vista getting ready to broaden yet again as I hummed to myself with a map of Rome spread in front of me. Bowen was in the small bedroom napping and the jet was on a course heading due, well, whichever direction the eternal city was in because we were going THERE next!

As usual, Claire hadn't given me much warning for this, but at some point a passport had been acquired and it had appeared in one of those folders in the car one morning. While C. and I were no closer in the friend department, she no longer snarled quite as hard when I messed up. It seemed that handling "the Colton situation" had given me some credibility with both her and Mr. Bowen. Claire had briefed me on where we would be staying (a small hotel on the square next to the Pantheon), and Bowen mentioned he would be cutting me some free time between meetings so that I could see the city, adding that a business acquaintance would be in Rome at the same time we would and that I might like spending some time with him. I would have strolled with Lucifer and Carol Channing as long as I was in Roma!

A car picked us up at the private airstrip; it was dusk, spatters of rain falling on a warm September evening. Ancient ruins were scattered along the main roadway like 7/11 stores were back home, electric lights and billboards jarringly out of place as the car sped us through the narrow streets.

"*Circus Maximus*, where the chariot races were held," Bowen said, with a nod toward a huge rectangular field filled with tall yellowing grasses. I had been horrible at history in school but this was living history and I nearly got an erection. Warming to his place like a tour guide, Mr. Bowen pointed out ancient *insula* (apartment houses) and even grabbed my head to turn it so I got a glimpse of the Coliseum in the fading afternoon light.

"Some place, huh?" my boss grinned. Even his rare white hot smile couldn't pull my focus from the beauty of this ancient city. I could only shake my head, eyes racing to take everything in as we wound through the streets, finally stopping next to the huge and ancient Pantheon.

It was Saturday night and Bowen said I was to meet him at ten AM Monday.

I knew the exact flight time between each of the cities we had traveled to on the Bowen jet.

I knew how much wood the fire places at Rose Bud would need for the winter.

I knew James' salary and how much celery Jean would need for the next six months for the menus he had presented me to consider I was learning stuff!

So you KNOW I had already looked up the gay bars of Rome....

I hit a couple, got seriously cruised and flattered. Bowen had warned me very sternly that there were guys who preyed on tourists, the unspoken text of what he said being that I should look and act like I had arrived by private jet and not tourist class on a discount tour, so I went back to the hotel jet lagged, alone and exhausted, but exhilarated.

The next morning I was up early and hit the dining room to wolf a huge breakfast. Somewhere between bites my telephone vibrated so I picked it up and read the text while minding for drops of jam.

The text message was from Bowen, who told me to meet him and his pal in the plaza at nine-thirty. Which I did, spotting the boss and his business associate, Calvin Harper.

If there was a model for the ugly American, it was Calvin Harper. There are physical things one cannot change – the fact that his ears stuck out like jug handles and that he was a head and a half shorter than me were just simple genetic facts. Along with the squinty eyes and braying laugh that cut through the air like a donkey that had just been kicked were just the physical attributes he brought to the table of bad taste that he was. His clothes added a level of unimagined horror to his being.

Here we were in one of THE fashion capitols of the world and this JHole is wearing: strappy leather sandals (well I guess when in Rome on THAT) in brown leather, black socks pulled up to his knees, cammo print cargo shorts held up by a wide woven leather black belt, and a T shirt (TUCKED IN!) emblazoned with *America #1!*.

Really, I kid you not.

All of this might have been more understandable if he had been over seventy. Or sixty. Or thirty even, but this dude was hardly over MY own age. Dressed better while not being attractive, he could have at least passed for cute, but in his current state he was making the hordes of poorly dressed tourists around us look great.

But Cal, as I was asked to call him, was pleased as punch to see me. Of course I am kinda easy on the eye – hey, look at me getting some self esteem back! And I was DRESSED, I mean I was in freakin' ROME and I had that whole kickass wardrobe at my disposal, so I had packed carefully and stepped out of the hotel wearing a pair of linen slacks (wheat), black loafers and a light Navy blue cashmere sweater that hugged my twenty-nine inch waist like it was in love with it. A crisp white button down shirt under the sweater made the tan I had bought from a tanning salon in the Pearl District of Portland pop even more. Armani (of course) shades over my eyes, I was hot on a fucking stick, in other words. Cal nearly broke into a jig on shaking my hand. By then I was starting to admit to myself that Mr. Bowen had a LOTTA guy friends who really liked the way I looked, but here in the square in front of what was possibly the world's longest running worship facility (some baaaaaddddd stuff had gone down in the very square we stood in involving the worship of God's before THE church stepped in and said wait a minute, a little less BLOOD and a few more RULES over on that side of the Tiber....), it was easy to overlook the fact that my "assisting" was becoming more "entertaining."

But I was in Rome and about to have some free time so time stood still, until Mr. Bowen saddled me with Calvin Harper of Shell Knob, Missouri, for the day.

After the introductions, Cal all but undressing me with his eyes and tossing me into that big skin covered X right there on the smooth stones of the plaza, Bowen said, "You fellas are going to have some fun today!" His smile was as bright as the morning sun was high over us and he looked almost human with the grin on his face. He was always handsome as hell, though. He was wearing a lightweight linen summer suit in charcoal, an open at the throat white shirt, D & G shades covered his sexy blue eyes. Standing next to him, I could see people of both sexes eye us for the couple we should be. But this would not be our Christmas card moment.

"Could I talk to you for a minute, Wyatt?"

Does the Pope wear a pointy hat? I thought but, did NOT say, just followed the man responsible for me BEING here a few steps away from Cal, who in the brief moment of meeting him had referred to the people of this beautiful and cultured land we were in as "eye-talians." The fact that Mr. Bowen had said my name almost playfully meant he must be very relaxed himself. Perhaps Claire kept a container of Xanax filled for him as well.

Using a move that would have made street magician David Blaine proud, Mr. Bowen managed to produce and transfer to me a small pouch. I slipped it into my pocket without even being told to. I was getting the hang of this "one step ahead" assistant thing.

"A bonus. Cal's family hit natural gas under their property some years back. He is a client and a good friend. Show him a nice day."

Words that would later haunt me like they had been uttered by Casper the friendly ghost.

But right then? I was in Rome, dressed like a model (okay, a print model), knew where the gay bars were and it was a beautiful day, so I was going to make the most of it.

Bowen gave Cal a hearty slap on the back and winked at me as if we were buddies and I was not on his payroll, and like a puff of smoke coming out of a Vatican chimney he disappeared and my day with Cal began.

Sigh.

Did you ever try to enjoy sightseeing with a pebble in your shoe? It is uncomfortable even after you stop and dump the pebble, then readjust your footgear. It's like you can still feel it in there.

The pebble that Cal Harper was quickly grew into a wolverine gnawing at my toes.

"Well, ain't he a member of the teeny-weeny-peeny club!" he said of statue after statue, ignoring the perfection of the lines and curves made by the sculptor's hands.

"These steps is just too dang wide!" commentary on a wide, low staircase designed by Michelangelo to make it easier for carts to navigate up and down a hillside to a wide plaza.

"Tell you what, they need some trucks over here, get some haulin' done then!" on traffic made up of Vespas and tiny cars zipping around the city.

I wasn't angry; if he was a client of Bowen, he was by default someone who helped my paycheck and I was not on personal holiday, so I took the commentary with as much humor as I could.

We were about two hours into our day tour, walking down a long narrow street filled with vendors and café fronts, I was trying to keep my mind in a happy, happy place, when I locked eyes with one of the sexiest young guys I had ever seen. He smiled and I smiled back, the *green light!* smile of hook-ups international.

"I am Matteo, may I offer you gentleman a tour?" he said in perfect English, brilliant grin

JAMES BROCK   93

returning to tell me that at some point we were gonna SEAL that deal. Despite that he was suddenly sandwiched between two amazingly hot men, Cal could not help a lifetime of ingrained wariness and rudeness.

"Now hold on here, how much is this gonna cost?"

"My treat, Cal," I said, the bundle of bonus Euro all but burning a hole in my pocket. I had intended to add it to my private bank but would have gladly blown the whole bundle to have wrapped myself around the hot Italian right then and there.

"Well, how do we know he knows what he is talkin' about?"

I could not have cared less if he had just made shit up, but at the question the handsome young man produced a small card of certification issued by the city of Rome stating that he was an accredited tour guide for the city. Handing the card over to Cal for inspection, he gave me an imploring look with those smoky bedroom eyes, a look that made his body the only thing I wanted to tour but I knew we couldn't just ditch Cal so I could take him back to my room.

"Well, guess it couldn't hurt," Cal said, as he handed the card back to the sexy Italian while mentally stripping Matteo and throwing HIM to the cobblestone walkway.

Well! How quickly I had been tossed over! But I had the solace at least to know that moments later from the gleeful look on his face, Cal had again mentally stripped me and tossed me to the ground next to our new tour guide.

The day got considerably better after Mattey joined us. Oh, Cal still made rude comments in the Pantheon (Call this a church? Why it ain't even got a whole roof!), referred to St. Peter's as where "them devil worshipin' boy diddlers" lived, and even made snarky commentary about Fontana di Trevi; "water looks dirty."

But all of his words were muted out by both Mattey and me, as we only had eyes for each other. If we were back in Portland I might have said it was love at first sight; we couldn't keep our hands off of one another. He stroked my arm in a cathedral in front of another Michelangelo sculpture; I brushed up against the smooth strong muscles of his chest in a tomb under the Vatican. Luckily for us, Cal was just happy to be along to have someone to talk at. He was the kind of guy who would have happily talked to someone deaf just as long as he was leading the one-sided conversation.

Mattey took us to a small off the tourist track restaurant for a lunch with several courses, including a small serving of me falling in a little bit of love with our guide. While the food was amazing, Mattey and I spent more time communicating our desire in silence than eating. Not that Cal noticed. He droned on and on like a tiny fly but did not seem to catch on that we were not paying any attention as he continued his slash and burn parade of insults to Italian culture. I had the feeling that he would have been just as rude were he in Osaka, Ontario, or Ohio.

Mr. Bowen had called me in to play with Cal at nine-thirty AM. We met Mattey two hours later, our long luncheon was followed by a tour of the Appian Way, Senate house and Capitoline museum, and dusk had long settled in by the time we left the buildings crammed with history.

"Well, I don't know 'bout 'chall, but I'm hungry for some real food. Let's eat at that MacDonald's we went by."

A chill of horror went through me.

"Come, I know another wonderful place for you to refresh with a light dinner," Mattey laughed.

"Light re past hell!" I want a burger from Mickey D's!" Cal was genuinely annoyed.

"Whatever your pleasure," Mattey said, with grace.

At the universal golden arches, we all stopped, then Cal turned to enter.

"Well c'mon fellas! This one's on ME!" he beamed.

"Actually, Cal, it's been fun," I said, with as much kindness as I could, "but I think I'm going to turn in.

Realizing I was giving him up, Cal turned to Mattey, who just smiled.

"How 'bout you and me breakin' some bread then?" There was nearly a hint of desperation in his voice.

"Thank you, no," Mattey said. The three of us stood looking at each other for a moment before Cal shrugged and went inside while Mattey and I turned and crossed the plaza back to my hotel.

Where we did not have sex.

Right away at least.

We made out. The young man's lips were as soft as I had imagined them to be all day. We teased, taunted and rubbed up against one another for a long while, then slipped back out into the square and we hit the clubs of Rome.

Hard.

There was kissing that grew more and more intense as we slipped in and out of each body packed venue, our hands roving up and under each other's shirts, trailing over each other's body until we were more than ready to be someplace private. Mattey's English was far better than my Italian, but we were speaking the eternal language of lust.

Back in my room we fell onto the bed fully dressed, making out again and the last romantic thing I thought before the carnal/sweaty stuff took over was this guy was one I could fall for if he lived just a kilometer or two closer to Portland.

SIX

I woke expecting Mattey to be in my arms. Or at least still in bed with me, but neither was true. And fudge was it light out! I was religious about setting my alarm, but being that I had my hands and arms filled with hot Italian I'd overlooked that little detail of my bedtime routine.

Squeezing my eyes tight, I counted to three and let them pop open before turning my head toward the nightstand where the numbers NINE-TWO SEVEN glared at me in red from a digital clock. The telephone sat in conspiratorial silence letting me know I had not done my hotel back up of calling the front desk for a wake-up call either. I was so fucking late it was not even funny. Calling out, thinking Mattey was in the bathroom, I waited but the resounding silence from that area told me he wasn't there. Head throbbing, body pleasantly tingling from our night of wild, passionate sex, I stretched, then moved to pick up the clothes I had left on the floor, and chair, and dresser. While still fully naked, half hard cock tingling, I lifted the jeans I had worn the night before and instinctively plunged a hand into the pocket. Empty. I wasn't looking for anything in particular, just doing a little paper trail reminder of the night before. It was amazing how easy it was to track myself from the trail of receipts I crammed into my pockets as I moved from bar to club to ATM machine to restaurant to back home. Without those reminders that I had done some drunken withdrawing, I never would have been able to keep my check book in balance.

The next pocket was empty as well. Not like me to not have hamster-like stuffed something in my pocket; a flyer, condom packet, flap of matches. Trash sentimental me might think a memento of the evening. As if the memory of being pile driver fucked by a smoking hot young Italian were not enough of a memory.

Frowning, I rooted back through both pockets like something was going to appear ala a magician's change bag, but they were still empty.

Surveying the dresser I found nothing there as well; no crumpled receipts, loose Euro coin. In fact, my watch, the silver chain I had worn around my neck, and my wallet were all gone. Stomach knotting, I literally leapt to the closet and felt like I had been hit with a hammer when I saw the safe door was wide open. I didn't need to reach in to know it had been emptied but I did. And I was right. There was only a dark void where my small stash of cash, a handful of Euro and my passport had been only a few hours ago.

Fuck. We'd had such a good time! Mattey had not seemed the thieving type. The hot, sexy type yes; a thief of my heart certainly. Sadly, I was more upset that he was just not there than the fact that he had taken my stuff.

Standing, still bare ass naked, I thought of the bonus cash I had been given and ran to the bathroom. When Mattey and I had come back into the room after leaving Cal at the McDonalds I had, with no thought that I might be getting ready to hang out with a petty thief (trust me, I had hung with worse....), pulled the packet of Euro Mr. Bowen had slipped me and stuck it down under a nest of damp towels I had left on the floor. My heart fluttered as my fingers grazed the pouch and I pulled it out. Dampish, but still there. Buck, Yen, Mark, Pound, Euro-Money, Money, Money as the song goes. I was without passport or ID, so if Bowen decided to drop my ass here I was sunk and would need to make this little bit stretch.

Now panic set in; robbed, still naked and late for my first ever Bowen meeting. Tearing through a shower, I started dressing, no time for the dining room breakfast; I was still buttoning, tying and zipping in the wheezing elevator on my way down to the lobby. The front desk called for a cab and I slipped in, handing the driver a sheet from my instruction packet (didn't skip reading THOSE since the first day) that had the address of the meeting on it. The meeting I was supposed to meet Mr. Bowen in front of the hotel to go to some time ago.

The small car screeched away, maneuvering through the narrow streets, nearly scraping against the ancient stone of the buildings around us. The car screeched to a halt in front of a sleek, modern building. I tossed a wad of Euro to the driver and bolted inside to the reception desk, where I was informed by a glaring receptionist, coldly and in perfect English, that Mr. Bowen had requested I wait for him out here. Rising slightly from her space age looking chair, she pointed a looooonng blood red fingernail toward a beautiful brown leather (Italian, of course...) sofa. Like a kicked puppy, I didn't question her, just crossed the room and planted myself, and settling my folder onto my lap, I crossed my hands over it. No reading magazines, pacing humming or counting floor tiles. I had effed up big time and telling Mr. Bowen about the heist in my room was only going to put the cherry on the cake of my day.

Over an hour later, my back aching and burning with shame every time the receptionist looked over at me, I was about to cross my legs to keep the circulation pumping when a sleek door in the side of the room opened and men filed out. Mr. Bowen and Cal were about third and fourth in the line. My boss of course looked like he had stepped off the cover of a business magazine – his dark blue suit with tiny white pin striping was perfectly cut for his lean muscular body. He wore a blue and grey striped tie over a crisp white shirt, hair slicked back he looked like perfection on a stick and I would have gotten hard had I not had such a ball of horror churning in my stomach. He looked at me, the corners of his mouth hitched down. Sweeping his eyes on me, he looked through me as if I were not there. Several of the men stopped to chat in a small knot while Bowen turned his smile back to the receptionist.

Cal, at least, had a suit on that fit even if it was the color of a faded dust bunny and his tie mustard yellow.

"Well, there you are!" Cal beamed as I rose, offering him my hand. At least someone was glad to see me. "Say we seen some stuff yesterday, didn't we?" Turning from me, Cal shouted toward Bowen. "Y'all boys wanna grab some lunch? I don't think we are far from that MacDonald's," he said in all sincerity.

"Sorry, Cal, we have to get back home," Mr. Bowen said with a smile to the client followed by a scowl at me. Handshakes all around were followed by Bowen turning to leave the room with me as his shadow. We went out to the car waiting for us in the plaza in silence.

"Mr. Bowen, I," I started. He held a hand up in that silencing gesture.

"Winners train, losers explain."

A commercial perhaps, but no arguing the logic.

"All you had to do was be nice to Cal. He almost didn't sign because you couldn't spend a few hours with him."

"I'm sorry, Mr. Bowen, I don't understand. I thought we did have a nice time," I managed to stutter. I had no idea what my being nice to Cal had to do with the business we were here on.

"Cal is an important client with Bowen and this was a major deal. He is rough around the edges, so part of your job is to be even nicer to clients who might need some special attention. I do take responsibility that I should have warned you not to hire one of those street urchins who fob themselves off as guides, but I thought you were coming along and could figure that out. Cal said you spent the entire day focused on the one you hired and left him to fend for himself."

"Mr. Bowen," I started, catching myself. The whole winners train/losers explain thing. We rode in silence for a few more twists and turns, but I knew I did have to speak out soon or we would be back at the hotel. "There is one more thing. I got ripped off. Matteo, the guide, stole my passport and some other stuff."

I have never seen a head turn so slow and careful. Words were not needed. William Bowen was seething. Handsome, but seething. He didn't say a word, just opened his cell phone as the car pulled up in front of the hotel.

"Go pack for both of us. The car will be back for you in two hours. Do not be late."

His icy words dripped acid. We had been in the city for three days but a seasonal change had happened. Our honeymoon was over, the spring thaw of our work relationship turned to arctic winter.

But it at least sounded like I was going to get to go home and not spend the rest of my days wandering the city begging and licking discarded wrappers from the "Mac Donald's" on Pantheon square.

Exactly two hours later, stomach churning, I had quickly and carefully packed for both of us and checked us out. I was waiting in front of the hotel when the car pulled up.

The driver stowed the luggage and I slid in. Mr. Bowen said nothing, tossing my passport, wallet and jewelry into my lap as the car started speeding through the crowded, narrow seats.

"I've had him beaten. When he steals from you, he steals from me. You are in another country and do not understand how things work here," Bowen's voice took on a deep, low tone. "You have been told you are the face of Bowen, my right arm. Destroy the dignity of that again and you are out. Understand?"

I didn't condone what Matteo had done and was sick that I had even put him in that kind of position. He saw me as a rich American. He didn't understand that I understood how difficult his life as an itinerant street guide must have been, but it was too late to let him know. And, too late to have a beating undone. I wanted to be sick but managed to blink back the tears that were welling up in my eyes and said, "Yes, Sir."

"We have a stop," Bowen's voice dripped with venom.

The car eased into a tiny parking slip; Bowen got out, with me following him into a building with a huge dark vestibule and up a long staircase. We entered a vast room filled with bolts of cloth and mannequin forms. A tiny man with a frizz of grey hair approached Bowen as if he were a long lost son. The pair embraced, Bowen nodding to me. The next thing I knew I had been led to a three panel mirror and was on a small raised platform while the tailor quickly streaked a worn measuring tape over my body as I realized I was at the holy of holies when it came to Bowen clothing – his personal Italian tailor was making me over. Which must mean that he wasn't going to fire me if I were being personally fitted. Bowen said nothing to either of us, he and the older man embracing as we left for the airport and a long, long quiet trip back to Oregon.

Back in Portland the car dropped Mr. Bowen at Rose Bud, then took me back to the wrong side of the tracks, that bad neighborhood I still lived in where it was easier to get crack than cappuccino. I didn't know what time it was and didn't care. While I hadn't been fired and evidence pointed that I wouldn't be, I was making the biggest decision of my life so far. Even if Bowen didn't call me in and formally end the job in the morning, I had reached a cross road.

I could not have anticipated what Bowen wanted me to do with Cal, or how to entertain him. There had been no handbook and while I knew I had come a long way (and that jobs were tight everywhere), what happened to Mattey was wrong and even if I wasn't let go I didn't know that I could continue trying to figure out what it meant to be William Bowen's assistant, other than that it was feast or famine, good times or bad times, with not a lot of grey area. The perks were fun (and profitable), but I couldn't condone someone being hurt because of me. I had gotten used to regular food and that regular paycheck and hadn't shopped at the broken food store in months, but I did keep that recipe for stone soup at the back of my mental file just in case. Pouring a stiff drink, I sat weighing my life options for a long while before finally heading to bed.

The next morning I dressed in a suit I had bought myself, not as expensive as those I had at the office, but nice and more importantly mine. I had a cup of strong coffee in the kitchen while the two cheaters chattered about the dancing they had done and the clubs they had been in and how very, very much in love they were. Their amore made me ill and I wanted so much to drop the bomb that I had just spent three days in ROME and gotten laid by a statue-come-to-life hottie on them, but I just wasn't up to it right then. They kinda had control (not that they knew it yet) of my homeless or not situation.

Rinsing the mug, I put it in the sink, then headed to the office. I had made a resolve that it would be better for me to find another job than live with what had happened to Mattey in Italy. If Bowen would have someone beaten there, well then it was time for me to find another job and leave on my terms rather than Bowen's. I had that little stash of, well, fuck money, to see me though – much more than I had than when the bank axed me. I'd found and gotten this job and there would be others.

I strode through the reception area without a glance at Claire and moved on into Bowen's office. My handsome employer was sitting behind the same massive desk he had been sitting behind the day of my interview.

"Wyatt?" He was startled. Wow, guess this is what made him so important here at his own company, remembering the name of his assistant. I didn't say that, of course.

Slipping my resignation and key ring onto the desk, I gave Mr. Bowen my thanks, assured him the clothing would be returned cleaned, and finished with an apology and a thank you for the opportunity. And for recovering my wallet and newly minted passport (which I was keeping!), before I turned away and moved back toward the door. Bowen didn't say anything until I had my hand on the knob.

"I know the players in Rome," he began, "so he was easy to find. I cannot let what he did be overlooked. While I didn't have the authority to punish him, I was upset and needed to make certain you knew the gravity of the situation. I wanted to scare you some. I'm sorry."

I did stop at that.

"You are shaping up as a good assistant, aside from this; you are learning. I would like you to reconsider leaving. It's Wednesday, come back Monday and we'll start over again. In fact, here,"

Mr. Bowen pulled a drawer open and handed me a ticket, "I was going, but you go instead. Lady Gaga in Miami on Friday. You'll go on the plane. Claire," he said into the intercom, "I'm sending Wyatt to Miami. Call the condo and arrange things. And have a company issued credit card put in his name; he's going to need to wardrobe up." Clicking off the intercom, he said to me, "And don't forget a bathing suit or two." His smiled was a real, warm smile at that, the kind of smile that could make a schmuck like me start crushing on this fucker I worked for.

"And Claire," he continued back into the intercom, "Monday we're going to need to switch out a parking spot for the company car Wyatt is going to be issued. Please arrange that as well."

I'd like to say I actually saw his heart grow three sizes Grinch-like as he realized how handsome I was, how beneficial I was to both him and Bowen Industries (gumball machines? Fish lines? Jack Nicholson memorabilia? What big business DID Bowen do on these trips?) and that either of those were the cause for him seeming to NEED to me to be there. I'd like to say I sneered at William Bowen, calling out his arrogance in thinking I could be bought. I'd like to say I told him I was bigger and better than a company car with a gas card attached. I'd like to say I told him how horrible and rotten what he had done was. I really did want to quit and tell

William-hot-as-the-sun-and-richer-than-Richard-Fucking-Branson to take all of his things and shove them and then go back home and lived happily ever after with honor and dignity on stone soup. But I didn't have much of a home to go back to, and the lobster and private jet lifestyle I had been living had grown on me, so yeah, while not forgiving Mr. Bowen, I did accept his bribes and went on to be a little monster.

SEVEN

Okay, so I am shallow and cheap.

I also was zipped right to the airport and put back on the jet I had almost gotten off of forever and flown across the country in STYLE. I slept in Bowen's bedroom, watched a first run movie, and ate like a king. The whole time I was in flight it never occurred to me that Bowen may have needed me to stay on rather than wanted me to stay in his employ.

THAT thought came at a future date.

For the moment, though, I was taken to a high rise condo, another Bowen property we are to assume, got my shop on in the boutiques lining the street of the complex, then went back for a swim in the huge rooftop pool. From there, I had an expensive dinner and went out and jammed it in some clubs until after four AM, thoughts of Rome and Mattey and Bowen all driven out of my head when I brought home a perfectly formed Puerto Rican with a smile that looked like it was made of lightning. He also had a dick nearly ten inches long and we did it like, well, the horny dudes we were until long after the sun came up when he finally gave me a peck on the cheek and disappeared down the elevator. Which is exactly what I wanted because Mi-jami was chock a block full of smokin' hot 'ricans and Cubans and Caucasians and, well, men in general all ripe for the picking.

I took full advantage of the Bowen corporate card, filling a suitcase with some wonderful couture pieces including an amazing outfit for the concert. Everything was tight, including me by the time I got ready to go. I'd had another swim, followed by another great meal, had awesome sex with half a dozen guys from clubs, and Claire, I assume, had made certain my Xanax "prescription" had been full and waiting for me on the plane, so I was plenty mellow by the time a car picked me up for the concert. A note from the front desk had alerted me that this had been arranged to take me to and from the hotel. Since I had already SOLD my morals and soul, why not take advantage of the situation since it was being offered?

The black town car whisked me not just to the stadium but to a garage under it, stopping next to an elevator which took me right to the box level. I could hear the roar of the fans streaming in down below, but I was in a wide, quiet, carpeted hallway. The handler who met me led me not just to a seat or a VIP seat, but to a freakin' box with a view of the stage that made me feel like I was on it. The place was plush, in other words; leather lounge chairs, plasma television, bar tricked out with top shelf booze. The small room was again nicer than where I lived! And bonus! No exes or bestie exes hanging over each other like they were made of jungle vines. I made myself a drink and settled in.

The concert wasn't due to start for another half an hour or so, my drink was tasty, and I was just groovin' on the vibe when the door to the suite blew open and a familiar voice rang through the air.

"Well, howdy cutie!"

I would have been just as surprised if Santa and several of the reindeer had suddenly popped in, and I could have gone back to the condo, faked being sick, or called in a bomb threat. I could have done any of those things but despite his brutishness I was glad I did see Cal because I did feel bad about Rome. Not about his terrible manners or the way he dressed or blowing him off to blow Mattey, but because despite what had happened – that Bowen had been horrible to me (and Mattey) but because we were in ROME for fucks sake and poor sad sack Cal, despite the money he had, didn't know any better than to go to McDonalds. He had probably never had a date as hot as me, either; yeah, I'm gettin' my brag on, but truth is truth. He may have been some business muckity-muck but I had something he clearly wanted, too. Bowen had wanted me to be friendly in Rome, so here Cal was and it was my chance to be friendly, so boy was I friendly. Between my drink (strong!) and my pretty little pill or three, I was well lubricated and let the good times roll!

"Cal!" I called out as if he were my new bestie, and like that song says, if you *can't be with the one you love, honey, then love the one you are with*...there had been a long line of those at Bowen; hell, I was doing more sleeping with his friends than actual work it seemed. And getting paid for it! And had use of that private gym! Which meant I had a truly appreciative audience for my "body of work." So what the fuck! At least Cal was dressed decently that night in jeans and a tight t shirt that thankfully was blank and showed a nice body under the thin material. A baseball cap was cocked on the back of his head. I would have pegged him as more of a Garth or Reba kind of guy, but he seemed to know who the Lady Gaga was, so I played bartender, knocking the cap off a Bud tall boy and handing it over to him. We clicked a toast, then moved to the front of the box as the house lights dimmed and the opening act rocked the stage.

And you know what? We had a good time! Of course we (well, me) were boozed up and there was not the distraction of a hot Italian tour guide between us-and it was only me and Cal in the box, and the music was so loud I couldn't hear most of his insults, so yeah, we had a good time and when the show was over I let Cal follow me back to the car where we started making out and then we went on back to the condo where we had some champagne, looked at the view and yeah, I went to bed with him and rocked his world.

Back in Portland things smoothed out between Mr. Bowen and me. He stopped being so short and while he wasn't exactly friendly, I could tell that there had been a step forward in our relationship. Of course, he had done a horrible, horrible thing to make that step happen, but that paycheck of mine coupled with that car and gas card went far toward making that an easier pill to swallow.

Speaking of pills, I had gotten the hang of private flying and could have told Claire I no longer needed the always full magic bottle of happiness she kept me topped off on, but I was by then kinda popping them like M&M's whether I was flying or not, just to take the edge off my appetite and the day.

Between sleeping with the occasional client, I continued adding features to my job; crisp white freshly laundered shirts joined the ties at the ready in Mr. Bowen's office. I stocked a small bar in a corner of the office and he started having the occasional drink there with clients. I even started going to Rose Bud more often and helping James out. The funny and cute house manager and I were getting closer. Jean the chef and I, though, were still chalk and cheese. The new suits had arrived from Rome. I'd never be able to wear off the rack or JC Penny or Macy's again.

Life, while not perfect in other words, was at least good for a change. I had a nice umbrella of cash put aside, a secure if vague job at times with a hot if distant employer, a sex life that might not be the envy of anyone else, but it was certainly constant and keeping ME happy.

But the umbrella I had carefully put together was not going to withstand the monsoon that swept in right about then.

I was nearly to my car in the parking garage one Friday afternoon (makes me kind tingly writing that line; "my", "car", "parking garage"….) when Colton meandered back into my life.

I'd had a long day doing *"something close to nothing,"* aside from the hours I'd put in at the Bowen gym; the biggest decision I'd had to make was chicken or fish for lunch (fish) and Nordstrom or Saks to buy new socks. It was Friday night and I was meeting up with James at a club later. He said he had a surprise for me and I so hoped it wasn't some kind of hook up. James and I still didn't have that much time to hang on our own and I wanted to dredge boss information out of him even if it meant getting him so lit we had to cab his gay ass back to Rose Bud.

Those were the kind of thoughts roving through my head when I looked up to see the tall blond who had been evicted (by moi) from Shangri La-like-Rose Bud staring down at me from the shadows. I would not have been more surprised if a talking bunny had appeared and asked for a slice of carrot cake. Stepping from behind a column, Colton stared hard at me.

"What are you doing here?" Dumb question on my part.

"He would have married me if YOU hadn't come into the picture. Wyatt this and Wyatt that," he said in a sing song voice that broke slightly before he steeled himself and took another step closer as if he had a pair. "He hasn't called and won't take mine, so I can only guess that
YOU are doing him."

"Colton, I don't control William Bowen. No one does," I said, with more force than I thought possible. There was a pause; long enough that I could feel my hair and teeth grow before Colton smiled. Not in a good way.

"No, you aren't sleeping with him or you would have reacted. But you are the dumbest one yet." His smile turned into a smirk.

"But I didn't get thrown out of his house and life," Dumb? Perhaps, slow enough to SAY that out loud? Not a chance.

"Mr. Bowen has moved on, Colton. You should, too." That firmness was back in my voice.

"Does *Mr. Bowen,*" Colton's voice turned to acid rain, "know everything that was *NOT* on your resume?"

I fingered the key fob to the car in my pocket, not liking where this conversation was going.

"Nice car. Not as nice as the one I had to leave back at Rose Bud," the former Mr. Bowen said, drifting up against the vehicle. Bending down, Colton roughly pushed on the edge of the driver side mirror and peered at his reflection.

"What do you want," I managed flatly, while pulling the small fob up into my palm.

"You don't know Billy's board of directors, do you? They put up with a lot because he is the last Bowen and he brings in a lot of revenue and they need it. But they won't put up with everything forever. And they won't deal with anything that might tarnish the precious name of Bowen," Colton said from his relaxed lean against my car. Well, the Bowen car I was given to drive.

I moved toward the car, pressing the button to unlock the car, followed by starting the car.

"I know about the porn is what I'm saying," Colton said on noting the all but silent snap of the lock popping.

I froze.

Perhaps a conversation with Colton would be more informative than one with James.

I never thought about the images and certainly had never given them any consideration in connection with my job. And now there was all of the sleeping around I had been doing ON the job. I had signed a contract but I had not READ the contract. Was there a morals clause? Fuck, what if Colton did tell Mr. Bowen about the porn, or what if Mr. Bowen started talking to clients I'd slept with? I felt a knot in the pit of my stomach. It was one thing to have quit on my own accord or to have been laid off, but to go job shopping if I were fired was a whole new big bag of crap for me and there was no denying anything.

"What do you want?" I asked again, trying to keep my voice flat again, as flat as it had been the last time I had asked this question – of course then it had an entirely different meaning.

"I think you should buy me some drinks, to start." His eyes gleamed ferret like when he saw that he had something on me. There was no reason to lie because the movies were out there for anyone to see.

"No, I've got plans," I started, taking a step toward the car. Getting out of there was all I could think of right then.

"That's not what I meant," he said, as my stupidity caught up with me. Letting the fob fall back to the bottom of my pocket, I reached inside my jacket and brought out my wallet, pulling out whatever cash was in it. Might have been ten dollars, might have been two hundred; I really don't remember. I pushed the bills toward Colton, who took them and shoved them into his pocket.

That human ATM transaction finished, I stepped toward the car, yanking the door open.

"We aren't done." Colton hadn't moved away from the car. "We'll be in touch. You help me get back into Bill's good graces and I'll let you keep your job." The "for now" was implied.

Countering with silence, I eased down into the leather seat, slamming the door and revving the engine as I jolted the gear shift into reverse and started backing out as Colton finally turned and slipped back behind the column he had been hiding behind. I held myself in from squealing the tires. No need to let him know even in a nonverbal way that I was upset in anyway.

Now I was out of the frying pan and into the fire, as it were. While I had been saving the money I made in my various capacities at Bowen both on and off the clock (hey I'm not judging YOU), I knew with Colton's champagne taste, my beer bottle pockets wouldn't go far. Especially if Colton decided to kill the golden goose (well, me...) and just tell Bowen about my little cinematic career to get back into his good graces. None of this should have bothered me, the guy who handed in a resignation not that long ago, but it did. Now that the initial shock was over, I was angry along with every other emotion storming around in my head and heart, that Colton of all people would have any say over my destiny. It was one thing to quit (well to offer to quit) on my own terms, but to have that piece of crap have a say was unbearable.

Plowing my way through the Friday afternoon traffic, I mindlessly hit the highway and rolled, not caring where I went as scenario after scenario played through my head, Socks and meeting with James forgotten, and I kept a steady pace of sixty with Beyoncé at high decibels. I was nearly an hour north on Interstate 5 headed toward Seattle when my phone rang, startling me back to reality. Ignoring all of the state cell phone laws about not talking or texting while driving, I answered.

"Where ARE you!" I could hear the noise of a bar in the background. James did not tolerate tardiness, especially when he was off the grounds of Rose Bud.

"Sorry...," I trailed off, not knowing what to say. I wasn't ready to tell him that Colton was getting ready to clean me out, not that I didn't trust James, but the past I had never given any consideration to had suddenly caught up to me, smacking me between the eyes like I'd been hit with a block of concrete. I couldn't erase the downloads, couldn't go house to gay house and buy back DVD's. Pictures, it turns out, are indeed worth not only the thousands of words but probably millions of dollars I would never have. Colton had developed some tastes that were spendy. And that wasn't counting what I knew were going to be the cost of his drugs alone.

I wasn't in any mood to go out with James right then but I knew if I didn't go he would have a million questions, and I had no answers and a lot to figure out on my own.

"Getcher ass down here NOW, Chica," my nearing new bestie shouted through a cracking line. "I'm gonna call you every five minutes for half an hour, then I'm sending a search party and you do NOT want that!" Usually quiet and mild mannered James had clearly run the drink flag up some time ago. I couldn't avoid seeing him no matter how much Colton had thrown me, so with a sigh turned the car around at an overpass and went back toward Portland.

EIGHT

The club we had agreed to meet in was NOT the big dance club that attracted visitors from as far away as Seattle, San Francisco, Mars and several smaller planets. On weekends at least it seemed that some of the dancers had come from other solar systems. We were to meet at a smaller club I had not often gone to, not because I don't like live performances, but mainly because the little bar was a usual hangout of those exes of mine, boy and friend. Any time I got to avoid them was, well, taken.

The crowd was pumped and jumping, a dance mix blaring out onto the street as I forked over a cover fee and hand my hand stamped by the large drag queen working the door.

"Show starts soon, baby; better find a seat. And you got a fine one on you…..," s/he shouted at me over his shoulder as I moved through the mosh pit of weekend revelers filling the small club entry. Pushing my way through the flailing limbs of the crowd, I waited in line at the bar, ordering a club soda when it was finally my turn. Yeah, THAT is how upset I was. I was driving the company car and had evicted Colton over DUI charges not that long ago, remember, so was taking no chances. Years earlier I had perfected how to carry a drink through a crowded room without spilling a drop. Winding through the crowd with my elbows tucked in, I found a stool against a low counter near the back of the room and squeezed myself between the forest of people and up onto it. Though I would really rather have been most any place else except perhaps at dinner with Ann Coulter and Rush Limbaugh.

The house lights blinked, then dimmed, and the crowd finally settled into their seats when a tall drag queen who had also perfected the art of carrying a beverage without spilling it stepped up next to me, staring down the occupant of the stool next to mine until he wordlessly vacated it. The queen slid onto the stool, cutting her eyes at me.

"Hey, soldier, in town long?"

I gave him/her a weak smile. Normally there would have been a pithy reply and we would have had a few minutes of verbal sparring, then spent the evening giggling and drinking while making new friends like "Kitten Khalua", "Dewmi Longer", and "Glimmer McCormick." I loved me some drag queens but was off my game that night what with the new hole that had been pierced in my wallet. Opening my mouth, I gave a little half start at saying something when the blond with hair jacked to Jesus dropped a butterfly wing size eyelash wing and smiled.

"What DID take vous so long to get here," my ornately make-up friend James said from underneath his gay apparel. His face had been constructed into a modern art piece by Bobbie Brown and he was wearing a fashionable black mini dress that left one shoulder bare and the other was covered with a single bell sleeve that fluttered around his fingertips. The recognition of his voice finally gave away the mask as I stared at James, a smile playing over his glossy candy apple red covered lips. Extending a manicured hand, nails attached that looked like he had just been feeding on a freshly slaughtered sailor (and s/he might have been, I was late for our date. Remember?), James closed his eyes and spoke, "Jimmi Saint Rose, charmed."

I can assure you I was surprised for the second time in the last few hours. My friend knew how to run an estate and how to throw a curve! And thankfully, how to blend, blend, blend when it came to make-up. He also knew how to mix and match some chiffon, velvet and sequins while some of his drag contemporaries thought nothing of going out in a gingham posing strap and elbow length latex gloves.

Before our conversation could continue, the show started. Legendary club owner Dahl Baby came onto the stage in full cow gal drag yodeling live and lip syncing to a Dale Evans number before going into a Q & A of the crowed, where he came on to the straight men, paired up the single gay men, and offered advice to several bridal parties who had made Friday night before the wedding day at the club a local tradition for decades. The Dahl Baby was old enough to remember the great depression and still managed to wedge his feet into pumps six nights a week even though the heel had dropped from a 60's spindle to a 70's cork wedge down to the jewel covered flats s/he favored now.

The night wore on, bringing drag queens! Drag Kings! Wigs! Beaded gowns! Fake hair piled high on heads and chests! Vamping! Camping! Lip-syncing-good and bad, dancing and drinking; it was all there. Old queens, young queens, drag kings with dicks made out of socks. Fat queens, skinny queens, tall queens, short queens-everyone was having a great time. There may have even been fire eaters and bird callers doing acts but I was pretty mentally checked out there for a while, finding myself for the first time since coming to the city nearly longing for the farm. Yep, that's how much of a toll my little encounter with Colton had taken and how desperate I was feeling. Poor "Jimmie" was trying to be a good hostess to me while chattering with friends who were passing by us as he got into the spirit of the evening.

"Lighten UP, Bridgett! Let's see soma that smile and CHARM you usually give out like a free gift with purchase!" the drag diva bellowed at me over a Rhianna number as s/he snatched at the glass I held. "What are you drinking…Nembutal?" Taking a sip, a shocked look crossed his face, and s/he held the glass away from me. "That is nothing but WATER!" he sputtered, while quaffing his own jewel tone beverage as if to take the horrible taste out of his mouth.

I was forming a reply when I noticed them, yep, the dynamic due I lived with was across the room. In no mood to deal with that happy little clown car of love, I suggested to Jimmie that the night come to a fast close but he was still sputtering about the discovery that I was trying to go the night booze free, giving my ex and my ex time to spot us through the throng of people and begin weaving their way through the drag queens and admirers, a mixed bag of gay men and their female accessories, to get through to where we were sitting. They also had to navigate assorted dykes, tyranny's, lady boys, transfags, genderfucks – I certainly didn't understand all of the assorted sexes that made up the crowd and community.

The guys shoved through the post show melee, arriving just as one of three Brittany types fell onto me; the 6'2" queen apologized while groping my crotch as we untangled, I saw the fall as a happy accident and reason to avoid making introductions all around, but the move didn't work as my roomie exes started shaking Jimmie's hand like they were priming a pump-farm kid, remember. We had pumps and they needed to be primed. Jimmie had, sadly for me, already been primed with several of the rosy red drinks, the remains of one was swirled to the dregs in the bottom of the glass s/he held.

"Well, hi fellas," Jimmie flirted.

Yeah, ok, they were worth looking at and Jimmie/James did not know the whole score but jumping Christmas trees, this was getting out of hand! Parts of my life I never intended to overlap were doing just that, and I just did not need that on top of everything else.

Thing One and Thing Two, to the naked and unknowledged eye, were any old hot couple off the stripper pole, but to me they were trouble on a stick. Granted, given MY current situation they were, say, low on the trouble totem of my life, but still I didn't need any complications. I had already come close to effing up my new career in Rome and possibly by sleeping my way through the company client list, although I had some grey area on that one because most of that was extracurricular and on my own time, and now I was being blackmailed by my bosses ex because he knew I was a very low level porn actor

once-upon-a-time-when-I-was-starving.   I   had
already begun salivating when I saw rocks because
that was all I was going to be able to stock my pantry
with if I lost this job. The last thing I needed was to
have more of my personal life given out and over to
the keeper of the Rose Bud keys, Jimmie Saint Rose!
I liked him, yeah, but still didn't know him or trust
him well enough to let him know that much about
me. While I finished lifting the drag queen off of my
lap, Jimmie and the exes had connected, and I next
learned that he had already gained new intel on me.

"You sly boots! Keeping it a secret that you
live with these precious boys!" Without waiting for
me to reply, Jimmie snagged a passing waiter dressed
as Joan Crawford in *Mildred Pierce* and circled a
long lacquered fingernail toward the beer bottles held
by Cheech and Chong. He then lifted his own nearly
empty oversize martini glass and bellowed, "Another
round, my good woman, and bring HER," with a
thumb jerk toward me, "anything with a lotta booze
in it!" I didn't argue, knowing I needed some
fortification about then. If Jimmie was connected
with the terror twins already, who knew what
direction this floor show would take?

I wished for lightening to strike me, him, them-
didn't really matter at that point. Any old disaster,
natural or otherwise, that would keep this
conversation casual and away from my personal life.

"Shame on you, Wyatt, not telling me THESE were the two fire hot boys you live with! Oh, the eye candy you must have around that apartment! I bet you two like to wrestle in jock straps, huh?" This broke Abbot and Costello into a fit of laughter.

"Sometimes," the ex Mr. Me said salaciously, "bet YOU could shed some light on what kind of work our Wyatt is doing and who it is for, too," he said, while leaning in toward Jimmie slightly. I remembered the move from our first date, how my blood had thrummed in my veins as the attractive blond then leaned in closer a second time, letting his soft lips brush against my arm. I'd been very closed mouth with the two of them about what I was doing and intended to keep what little time I might still have with Bowen quiet as possible.

"Who was the guy doing Madonna? Wow, I would have sworn it was really her," I inserted to Jimmie, only to be rewarded by stares from all three of them. They were not buying my attempt to change the subject.

"You were talking about Wyatt's work," the other one said, as HE leaned in toward Jimmie, who was all but eating the attention the two of them were giving him with a spoon.

"WE," the drag queen said with authority as the *Mildred Pierce* doppelganger reappeared, Jimmie expertly removing the bottles and glasses from the tray without tipping the tray, then snaking a hand down into his faux cleavage to fish out a wad of sweat damp bills, liberally sprinkling them onto the tray as he instructed the server to put the round on his account, "work for Bowen Industries," he continued, with a tip of his glass to us all. "I am in the housekeeping department while Wyatt is Mr. Bowen's number one, his aide-de-camp, lady in waiting and general all around gopher."

"THE William Bowen? I'm impressed Wy!" my ex said, in a way that I knew he meant it. While that old saying, *revenge is a dish best served cold,* may very well be true, the timing of my first slice could not have been worse. I was officially in a house of cards and anything along the lines of an, "I told you I'd make it and be better than ever!" at this point could easily bite me deeply in the ass. So I just smiled with as much noncommitment as I could while lifting the booze filled glass and draining it just as "Fauxn" Crawford slid another booze filled glass onto the counter next to me, Jimmie giving me the *"I told you so"* look that meant I would have a much better evening by adding booze.

Well, since that was the way the night was going to go, I dug deep into my pants (no, not looking for the good stuff that lurked below...) and brought out a pill, palming it expertly. I had gotten very good at making certain Mr. Bowen, the pilot,

Charlie, the hot flight attendant, or any of the sometimes not so attractive business associates I was getting ready to dive under the blankets with never saw me slipping one of my mother's little helpers. Giving the one I brought out a pop into my mouth, I lifted my glass and swallowed. Within a few minutes I didn't care as much, and another few longish drinks, and I was well on my way to not caring at all.

Including, I later came to realize, the fact that Jimmie Saint Rose had begun to round up a posse of party people including the Olson twins I lived with and was now directing them to a house party at the one, the only Rose Bud. I knew William Bowen would not be home (the fast little jet had taken him to Washington D.C. and he was not due back until the first part of the week).

James, of course, knew the boss' schedule, too, and for all I knew this was a regular thing, that there was a full-time Bowen sponsored and paid drag queen assigned to the front door of Rose Bud every Friday night, stamping arms and ushering the cool crowd into the vast living room with a wave of he/r bejeweled wrist. So I said nothing as Jimmie/James handed out verbal invitations (faster than e-vite!) to an after-hours soiree. I should point out that between the booze and pills (yup, there had been a tiny few more….), I was a case study for *Valley of the Dolls*

Two and should have not been held accountable for my actions.

As an adult, employed and keeping a roof over my head, I should have told Jimmie/James *NO!* That Rose Bud was OUR place of employment – well, I had a hand in there somewhere – and that this impromptu event that was seeming to celebrate putting all of the pieces of my life together in one basket was not going to happen.

But I didn't. It all happened so fast and I was so drunk and looped out of my head, the lights had melted into a dreamy blur, the music had me riding on a river of comfort and for the first time since Colton stepped out from behind that pillar, I was relaxed.

I also did not know that Jimmie had a slightly tougher edge than just plain James. The resourceful drag queen had slipped a little something to our server, the homage to the star of *The Women* and *Whatever Happened to Baby Jane,* along with a moist handful of tips, to not only give me 100 proof vodka but a little vial of powder to pour into my drink. So booze, prescription drugs, and some kind of big cat tranquilizer were coursing through my veins, veins that had been used and abused but were at that moment taking a vote as to whether or not they wanted to stay in my body or just migrate out en masse in protest to what was being done to them. I somehow left the bar and ended up at the casa de la boss man.

I don't really remember how I got back to Rose Bud, or even which door I came through, but there was no drag queen stamping anything anywhere, although there were a number of them smoking on the front lawn and two were wrestling what appeared to be some sailors or marines who had been imported for the event on the long white sofa in the living room. The one now marked with several sweaty pit stains and streaked with two shades of lipstick.

Not that I cared, really, I thought, as I staggered toward the bar; the house was still Jimmie Saint Rose's responsibility. And about that time the "lady" of the house in question appeared, hugging me, then pushing me farther into the living room just as the sound system began blaring one of my new favorite songs.

"Show us what you are made of, baby!" James encouraged. In his defense, he had put away a gallon or so of something distilled, so was not in the total control he usually was.

"Yeah, dance man, dance!" my ex shouted from the sofa where he was tangled with the former bestie and perhaps a paratrooper.

So I danced.

Meaning, I gyrated, rotated and yeah, started peeling off clothes. Layer by layer and sexy as hell –

not that I remember but I had been doing all of that working out and knew the particular crowd I was with was enjoying what I had to offer by the noise they were making – the very good kind of noise complete with hoots and cheering. They were in fact enjoying my show so noisily that none of them heard the front door open and close for someone just now joining our new early morning soirée.

Down to my underwear, a particularly tight and low cut pair of briefs, one arm lifted high above my head with the other shoved deep into my crotch, eyes closed and head thrown back, I was hot and knew it. In my groove, I snapped my face down to the roar of the crowd while using my thumb to roll the band of my underwear down to expose my thick black pubic hair. Opening my eyes, focus being a challenge at that point, I found myself face to face with William Bowen.

No one else in the room, of course, knew who he was. My freezing suddenly in place should have told them something, but the crowd wanted me naked, two drag queens who would never again see size sixteen dressed jumped up and were about to peel my underwear off like I was a boiled shrimp when James came roaring into the room. He had managed to strip out of his drag and was now in a pair of tight jeans and a pink polo, his feet in penny less penny loafers and face scrubbed clean of the peacock colors and glitter he had been wearing.

"Mr. Bowen! Is everything alright?" I heard James exclaim as the drag duo holding onto me let their hands drop as the music came to a sudden halt, the crowd catching on that this was an unauthorized event that was coming to a sudden end. Oh, trust me, this was not the first time this crowd had gotten the old heave ho from a party. For most of them it wasn't even really a party, in fact, unless it ended with them on the lam.

I didn't hear an accusation of "he did it!" from James, the now former Jimmie Saint Rose who held a quick time record for reverse drag removal, but as the guests were being chased from the living room and vestibule by the very host/ess who had only hours earlier invited them over, I did hear some sordid little tale of him being in town with his sick mother and getting a call from gate security that there was some kind of wild party going on at Rose Bud.

There was nothing, however, I could do to stop his Tennessee Williams like romantic fictional account of his evening with his mother, as my vocal cords had gone on strike it seemed, along with my dignity, so I just slumped down onto the already soiled sofa. I felt no shame being there in public, lights blazing in the big room, in my skimpy underwear. I didn't either try and chide James or explain anything to Mr. Bowen. The facts were there and I was so

drunk and pilled up I couldn't get my tongue muscles to work if I tried.

I did try to get up, though, but stumbled, so decided to stay put. Eventually (ten minutes? an hour? two days?) time passed and just before I passed out, Mr. Bowen and James came back into the living room. Hooking their arms under mine, how James had sobered up enough to pass as NOT DRUNK was amazing; it was like a bucket of cold water had been thrown on him, the two men wordlessly hauled me through the house to the guest suite.

As they parted in the hallway after tossing a cashmere throw over my ripped, muscular form, neither James/Jimmie Saint Rose nor I saw the smile that crossed William Bowen's face or heard him mutter, "Good night, my little money machine," as he swept down the wide corridor of the second floor of Rose Bud and on to his master suite at the end of the hall.

NINE

I woke like a vampire. One minute there was nothing, then there was the world and light and a wrenching in my gut like I had never felt and the noise! SO much fucking noise! I heard beetles, walking, water dripping in a rain forest-I think I heard a faint conversation being held by my parents down on the farm in the southern part of the state. Luckily I was numb, feeling nothing other than nausea. Which meant I didn't at least feel the shame or humiliation I should have been feeling. Slivers of the last fifteen hours began flickering through my brain. Colton, drag queens, booze and pills-ending with me in my underwear in the middle of William Bowen's living room while face to face with William Bowen. I had no idea how I got onto the big soft bed I was in the middle of, but was relieved I still had my underwear on.

"Wakey wakey! Egg's and bakey!"

James came through the doorway; I smelled food and felt another wave of nausea.

"C'mon, sunshine! Jean's made a big breakfast fit for a queen, so sit up and start with a sip of juice. It's got a little vodka surprise in it….," the traitor trilled in a stage whisper. Taking a deep breath, I let a hand slide out from under the thin throw over my shoulders, exposing my barley covered ass cheeks while I peeked around for something to throw at James.

"Here," he finally said in sympathy after sliding the tray onto the edge of the massive bed I was on as he tucked something into my curled fingers that felt like a television remote. "Oh, baby, would you like me to just throw it at myself?" I tried to nod but felt like my head was going to fall off my shoulders. Pulling the remote from my fingers, James grabbed me, flopping me around like a rag doll until he had me pinned up against the headboard. I still couldn't vocalize. Glaring was the mot I could do, but I did have a good one of those going as James deftly lifted the orange juice to my lips. Gagging at the smell, the overwhelming sweetness of the juice covered by the raw stink of alcohol hit me like a fist, but I let him get a good slug down my throat before I pushed him away, managing to take the glass first.

"What the fuck, dude!" My voice was back! "Sold me down the fucking river!" I sputtered, head spinning.

"I know baby…," James trailed off, lifting a crisp strip of bacon off the tray and nibbling at it, "but there was no sense in ME catching the heat since YOU are his little A #1 Superstar. He LIKES you dude and I have never known him to like one of his assistants."

A thought formed like a bubble in my head, the words rose and exploded out before I could slam another jolt of the drink into my face.

"This has happened before, hasn't it?" I managed, then took another fast drink of the mostly vodka filled glass, my eyes again squinted shut against the light and the gravity of my situation.

"Look, we can dwell on the past, point fingers," James said, while plucking up a slice of bacon off the plate.

"Throw friends under busses….," I said, reopening my eyes.

"But really, what good is any of that going to do? I say we form a plan and move forward."

"Yeah, but the plan I am working under includes being fired and probably legal charges being levied," I countered, taking a sip. Whew. The strong brew was reviving me, well refreshing my drunken stupor.

"Do you want the truth?"

"No, let's stick to fabrication and fantasy. Please, please, please lie to me." Staring blankly at me, James finished the slice of bacon and wiped his fingers on his jeans. I had another sip of the by now delicious beverage as *Tell me all your secrets and I'll tell you most of mine,* the theme of a television show played through my head. After the way he had let me take the fall for the party, I was in no mood to open up to James about everything going on in my world.

"Well. I don't plan to be a property manager forever."

"But you have such a career holding this bouquet of Roses together," I snarked, before draining the glass. The morning was turning into a vignette by Edward Albee.

"Aren't you clever," he intoned, "and stop it! Oh, he pays well and I know my way around a budget and some estate management, but Dahl Baby wants to retire and has offered to sell me the club! I'm doing up a business plan to present to Bowen because I'm going to need some deep pocket backing. Jean is coming with me to run the kitchen; it's going to be fab!"

I could tell James was serious, so I put the snark on hold while he went over the details.

"And why was throwing MY reputation out the window the way to make this happen?"

"Hes like you, stoop. I've never known him to like a real person like you; he generally goes for knock off people like that horrid Colton."

"Has he TOLD you he likes me?"

"Not in so many words, but he hasn't fired you and you haven't quit."

"The day isn't over yet," I sighed. It was actually comforting to know that James at least had a plan and exit strategy. If I lost this gig, my best bet would be to force James to hire me as a server in his drag bar. Even if Colton and Bowen got back together and came in every night to check the club take like the owners of a 1930's gangster movie, they would never spot me in my clever diner server drag. I would base my character on that of Ida as played by Eve Arden in *Mildred Pierce*, the tough yet tender Vi as played by Joan Blondell in *Grease* and I'd throw in a good dose of Alma, the feisty housekeeper created by Thelma Ritter in *Pillow Talk* with Doris Day and Rock Hudson. If I needed to ramp it up, I would go Alice by Ellen Burstyn in *Alice Doesn't Live Here Anymore,* and if I failed at the club doing that, well there was always dinner theatre doing revivals of *Annie Get your Gun.*

I would have to work on my language though. I've sworn like a sailor since about fourth grade and I wanted my server character to have a body that might have been tarnished by the wrong me she had dated but a heart of pure gold. If "her" mouth needed to be washed out every few minutes, it would diminish the quiet dignity and class I wanted to have.

"Oh, it'll be great!" James almost squealed with joy, digging back into the tray of food he'd brought for me.

"Where's Bowen now?" Another cocktail like the one I held and I'd be ready to make the presentation for James right then. Thankfully, my aching body and roiling stomach assured nothing like that was going to happen right then. For the moment, getting out of my stained (I was asking no questions on THAT front) underwear, cleaning up and recon on the boss was the best I could manage.

I was also strangely calm. Well, I was still drunk is what I was, but now I had a plan, structure, no matter that it was built on the foundation of being employed as a drag waitress in a pipe dream club.

Have you figured by now that the constant threat of stone soup was very, very bothersome to me?

"He left early," James said, as he deftly slid a fluffy biscuit around the plate to get at all of the greasy goodness of the meal he had prepared for me.

"Seconds after the party broke up? What was that, nine, ten AM?"

"Don't be so dramatic! It was much earlier than that; I think he rolled out around eight."

"So what do I do, call him? Wait for him to call me? I don't even know where my clothes are and nothing in here," I said, with a sweep of my arms around the room, "is mine except these."

"And adorable they are! Do you always wear skimpy little thongs like that or did you think I had more than a drink in mind since you knew you were meeting with me?" James leered while using the napkin to daub the corners of his mouth, then leaned back in a satisfied stretch. "Your clothes are right over there, laundered and ready." James had been a busy little home manager already that morning, between delivering and eating my breakfast and overseeing the woman who did the actual work in the laundry room. I suspected a nap was on his list of near future chores.

"Not that it is any of your business, but I usually wear boxers, never got much into briefs and usually by the end of the week I haven't had time to launder anything so am commando. Now help me help you," I said, while trying to push James off the bed.

"Keep those briefs on and your mouth shut. Don't call him. Don't bring it up – you have been with Bowen long enough to know that there are many things you don't ever need to discuss with him. If Billy wanted you out of here, you wouldn't have spent the night. Remember Colton."

"That would have me being thrown out of here by YOU."

"I would have done it with dignity, dear," James said, with a sweet pat on my shoulder. "Another bevie?" "I'm having one." With a nod, I slumped back against the upholstered headboard and closed my eyes. My head was thumping like a monkey was beating a drum in it. Feeling James sit back down on the bed, I put my hand out without looking and let him slide me a sweat beaded glass.

"I bet you are just adorable in those expensive custom made suits the days you aren't wearing undies," the houseman mused. I ignored the comment, but was ready to turn the snark back on.

"How long did some of the other assistants last and what were their downfalls?" I asked after a sip. James took a gulp of his drink and stretched out next to me.

"Well, I've never known any of them to go more than a few months, but then not all of them came to the house."

"Any reason for duties to change from assistant to assistant?" James just shrugged, his silence telling me no was the answer.

"Let's see, Adrian was a hottie just like you. Dark hair, scruffy beard. He spent a lot of time in the gym at Bowen. Dumb as a Cocker Spaniel."

"Hey! I spend a lot of time in the gym at Bowen and have known some pretty smart Cocker Spaniels," I protested, eyes still tightly shut.

"Daniel, well Dan as he insisted on being called, was a butch closet case but never came to Casa Bowen. Billy kept him in the office, but then he didn't last long either, couple of weeks. I never asked and he just stopped answering the phone one day. Very *Picture of Dorian Grey."*

All interesting to know, but no dish of value yet.

"Carlos was the import, said he was Spanish….," James trailed off.

"Hey, buddy, is that some prejudice showing there?" I cautioned.

"Please. Fucker was hot as the sun and bright as a creek rock…one of my favorite combinations."

"How long did he last?"

"Month or two."

"So how do you find out when a new assistant comes on board?"

"Claire runs that end of the operation. She calls and tells me when some hottie dude like you is going to show up for training."

"How does she feel about us…?"

"Don't really know. She is a lone wolf but I guess like the rest of us, she has hopes, dreams, fears, and likes to eat and have a roof over her head, so she does her job."

I had hoped a little history would help me know the true odds of being fired but none of this rotten information helped my current situation at all.

The rest of the restless weekend was spent not eating or drinking, unless you count water and power bars. My time was spent doing killer workouts on the treadmill followed by endless laps in the pool, pumping until my arms were numb. Mindless activity, save for counting reps. October 29, 1929 couldn't have been a blacker Friday than the one I had faced the day earlier. I knew what it was to be hungry and nearly homeless; fudge, it had been less than a year since I had done my last porn. In the current economy jobs just didn't fall off trees and I knew the threat Colton was holding over me could collapse my little world of creature comforts like food and shelter.

On the positive side of things, though, I had made a very smart deal with the devil move by staying in the tiny apartment living as Lady (well, me) and the tramps. And I still had use of a car which meant I could use the weekends to drive to Seattle, Vancouver, British Columbia and San Francisco if it came to doing movie or magazine modeling. Ok, ok. Porn, Sheesh. And perhaps, yes, just perhaps, if it came to it, "escort" work. While I didn't like the idea of it, the work still beat going back to the farm defeated or to the food bank.

The only other option I thought of in the face of my impending dismissal was finding one of those friends of William Bowen who seemed to like me so much to take me on full time. I had quite the network of guys who liked to wine and dine (and ok, nail) me that I could try to fall back on. I knew most of them were married and hated the idea of fishing around to be a kept guy but had, as noted, gotten accustomed to shoes and butter and meat and having a starch in my meals.

Of course, the unimaginable might happen and hot William Bowen might start flirting with me, which would lead to me moving into Rose Bud and doing charity work and hosting tea for the society of Portland. And if James gave me any lip, then I'd have a fun little maid uniform made up for him to wear.

Golden handcuffs firmly locked in place because I couldn't quit now and didn't have anywhere to go, I went back to work Monday, hair neatly combed, smile fixed and as Mae West said, continued to *"Climb the ladder of success wrong by wrong."*

The morning was quiet. I kept waiting for the axe to fall. Mid morning, Claire directed me into Mr. Bowen's office.

"Friday night never happened," he said, after having me sit down and giving me a long, quiet (uncomfortable as hell) stare. "Keep skating so close to the edge of the ice, though," Bowen said in a deadly tone, "and you just might fall in. Lotta guys out there looking for work."

"Well, there was a threat that didn't have to be written on a blackboard or sent via text. "I like you, Wyatt," high words of praise from the Easter Island stone head silent guy he usually was, "so get, and keep, your shit together."

I went back to my office to lick the verbal wounds the boss had just lashed over me, and pop one of my little happy pills, but I didn't have a lot of time to let it churn in my stomach, as a short while later Bowen and I were on the way to the airport. We strapped in and took off. I assumed there were pilots involved in our trips as handsome men in uniform were always milling around the doorway leading into the cockpit of the sleek little jet, but I never met any of them. Heck, there could have been an autopsy room or disco at the front of the plane for all I knew because I was never invited into that space. We arrived in New York, New York (of course, of course) in the middle of the night, a town car picking us up and on to the corporate condo on the upper west side.

I was relieved to still be employed, but figured Bowen had the office back in Portland filled with another batch of assistants-to-be, so I had a plan. Not a good plan but if you know nothing more than some superficial stuff about me, you should at least have it registered that I operate best with a life road map handy.

One of my former life drug supplier buddies still worked as an escort (I KNOW! Shocking!) and he had been in New York for awhile (my network kept me posted up on this kind of trivia), so I arranged to hook up with him to see what kind of career in that fast paced, fast money world might be left for me at my age. Which would be very short lived unless I hooked into the hoped for *Pretty Woman* deal. Which stood about as much chance of happening as a squirrel playing a concert at Carnegie Hall. Well, Liza had made a comeback or three there, but she had lineage to fall back on even with blown vocals. All I had to fall back on was my worked out body (that did look really, really good right then), but that shit wasn't going to be lasting once I lost access to gym time several hours a day.

TEN

Bowen had been deadly quiet on the subject of parties, while I was a little sensitive (ok, paranoid) on the topic and excessively concerned about my employment despite his words.

We settled into our suites and the next morning met after breakfast and went to our scheduled meeting. A rare" real" meeting complete with women and presentations and facts and figures, whatever Bowen did it was it was done in a big and global way.

There were no snacks to spill, no apologies (well, sex) to be given out as an "I'm Sorry" favor, so naturally I was bored out of my mind. I was no longer pretending to take notes and felt like I was only there as a hot looking accessory to make Bowen look good. I spent my time thinking only of meeting up with Randy later. He had been a cute, fun club kid when we met at that big Portland dance club a few years back. Once he had gone through the first wave of Johns in Portland and business dropped off after he was no longer the new meat in town, he moved; South to L.A., then east. I sent him a text as we left Portland telling him I would be in the city briefly and wanted to hook up, leaving out that I might shortly be unemployed and was testing the escort waters. I got a fast "Cool!" in response and agreed to meet him outside an Upper East Side club named *The Penthouse.* William Bowen and I would be heading to Denver early the next morning on that fast little jet.

I was going to miss that most of all. Oh, I would miss popping Xanax like M&M's and would miss the hot face of Bowen in the form of Mr. B., but that jet would be longed for.

There was a moment of hesitation at the end of the day when I thought Bowen was either going to tell me we were leaving for Denver right then or fire me, but neither happened. He left for dinner with a group from the meeting and I was on my own.

Changing into jeans and a t shirt, I grabbed a jacket and had a walking dinner through the streets of the city, grabbing a big sloppy slice and folding it in half like a true New Yorker as I strode the early evening streets like John Travolta in the opening scene of *Saturday Night Fever.* Finishing the pie, I grabbed an Italian ice (Lemon!) and had a fast beer at a little gay bar on the way and was still early when I found myself in front of the address of the bar where Randy and I had agreed to meet.

TAILOR MADE

It was still early, deep twilight, and I loved being there in the middle of the city and the attention the men going into and coming out of the bar were giving me. Correction, the older men were giving me. The younger crowd ignored me, even though I cop to being hot, some of them were smokin' and dressed to show it. The fashion watch word for the night was "tight"; pants, t shirts, even the shoes looked molded. There were punk types, construction types, pretty types, a whole *Village People* array of studs moving up the slight of steps into the crowded bar.

The first half hour waiting was not bad. I was getting looked at and hello'ed left and right. The next half hour with no sign of Randy, I sent a "WTF?" text and went inside where I got a drink and stationed myself where I could see the front door. And damn if the men inside were not even friendlier than those outside! They chatted with me, asked if I were from out of town, offered to buy me drinks. I felt like I was at work, I was so popular.

It was nearing the end of 90 minutes beyond the time Randy and I were to meet when a very charming and well dressed man who was old enough to be my grandfather leaned in over our drinks and in a jovial tone asked me to come back to his place and ram my arm up his asshole. Well, let me tell you, that told me a LOT about where I was. While I had indeed

JAMES BROCK   157

fallen off that turnip truck as mentioned, I was now in New York and dealing with a whole new level of vehicle to fall off of. While I was sophisticated in Portland and in the months of being aide du Bowen had learned a LOT, I clearly had a long way to go when it came to reading the obvious.

"Um, thanks, no," I returned. He countered by offering me a large sum of money. I don't mean a drink, I don't mean enough for dinner and a show. I mean a really nice sum of cold hard American cash. A sum I was startled by and considering (unemployment was looming, remember, and I HAD gotten tipped for "stuff" recently) the offer, when Randy came through the doorway. Rather stumbled through the doorway, literally. He would have had to do some work to have gotten back up to scruffy but he was still fuckin' hot. We said a brief hello and the next thing I knew Randy had maneuvered myself and the guy who had made the offer down the stairs to the lower floor; a darker, quieter version of the living room like atmosphere of the first floor. Well, living room if you were an alcoholic decorator who had installed a bar the full length across the back of your living room and staffed it with guys who looked like street hustlers.

Well, guys like Randy and me, hot in other words.

Randy and I did not chat up our past life; he lifted his arm to a waiter and ordered up a round of drinks. Bottled beer for him and me, a tonic and something for the guy we were with, who was clearly loving the attention of two sexy guys paying him attention. He and Randy appeared to be old buddies, my new pal leaning in and whispering sweet nothings into the ear of my old pal, both of them looking across the room and falling into a fit of giggles over a young guy they had both pointed at. The drinks arrived and it became clear that we were settled into the territory we had staked out on a long, curved (comfortable!) sofa for the long haul and that Randy and I were not going to have the quiet time alone I had hoped for.

I didn't mind that the older guy we were with was taking Randy's attention. Randy was clearly at work, I was still getting looks – well, looks from the other older men and glares from the younger guys who must have seen me as new meat competition. Which in a matter of hours, days or weeks I might very well be.

Handing my beer over to Randy to watch, I excused myself to the men's room. Which was a whole new adventure.

"Where ya from?" a slender blond in a black cowboy hat and tourniquet tight jeans asked as soon as I entered the small room.

"Uh, Portland." I might as well have said Needle Rock, Arkansas or Swamp Moss, Mississippi.

"Well, the guys are all talking. Keep away from the regulars unless you wanna split some fees," he said, while turning back to look into the mirror and adjust his hat.

"Listen, Midnight Cowboy, I'm just here to meet a friend and have a drink," I started, the faux cowboy staring at me in the reflecting glass above the sink.

"Uh huh, we are all doing that," he said flatly. "Randy has been known to bring new meat in to play doubles and that is sure what this looks like. And I ain't talkin' tennis."

"I don't know what you are talking about," I lied, "he just asked me to meet him here." I had figured out by then that we were in a hustler bar but I wasn't going to let this guy know I knew. And in case I did come here to sell my wares, I didn't want to offend anyone right off the bat.

"You wear that innocent look pretty well." Adjusting his crotch, he winked. "If you decide not to double up with 'ol Randy, look me up. We'd be a good team. I'm Ace." He didn't offer a hand but as he turned away, looked at me with a stunning smile and I realized he was 100% right. As a high end team we would be raking in the dough.

Back in our little corner of the (bar) world, the older man was lightly massaging Randy's shoulders. Randy handed me the beer bottle, suggesting I drink up because Gene wanted us to go back to his place for a real drink.

Life is full of choices, left/right, up/down, and as we grow up we are supposed to get better at making them. I had a job, a fairly impressive sex life, a company car and, oh yeah, a blackmailer on my ass.

Still even that didn't push me toward saying "Let's roll!" until Gene, our host with a plan for my hand, leaned over and whispered the number he had mentioned while we were alone upstairs. Before I became a working boy in that working boy bar. Reaching up, Randy slipped a tiny white pill into my hand. Smaller than an M&M but larger than MY pilly little Xanax buddies. It was a teeny A bomb for the brain I knew, no matter how innocent it looked. But what the fuck, I could nap on the plane the next day if needed.

Downing the pill with the dregs of my beer, I was feeling good before we were even out of the bar. I mean really good. Relaxed, warm, I cuddled against Gene as we moved onto the street and Randy expertly hailed a passing cab. Somewhere deep in my gut I knew horrible, horrible things might go wrong with this little escapade but the lure of that big money mixed with that little happy pill kept me going. And frankly, Gene did not look like a guy who lasted. There would probably be a first come-hard and fast-followed by a snack/drink/bathroom and nap break during which I could fit in a little business chat with Randy. And hit him up for a place to stay until I got established. Round two with Gene would be slower and after THAT Randy and I would likely get a little nap, followed by being paid and leaving. So the upside of the evening was that the work would be split and I would be leaving with a large sum of cash. Plus, I had never done anything with cute Randy and there was likely to be some sexual overspill, so score!

Onward and upward!

The ride in the creaky (but classy!) elevator (and there was of course a doorman) in Gene's building took care of the upward. By the time we reached the massive thick door of his apartment, a door so well made and hinged it could have come from any of the doorways at Bowen, I was feeling time expand and contract. The hallway seemed to telescope down to a pinpoint, then bounced back to a realistic length. That should have told me the pill was working just fine, and coupled with the beer and drink to come that I was flying as high as I needed to go.

JAMES BROCK   162

None of which explains why I accepted a second pill palmed to me by Randy while Gene was making drinks. The pill that clearly was the one that made me small Gracie Slick sang about.

The night still comes back to me in nightmares. Smeary, blurry nightmares that leave me coated in sweat. There may have been physical contact with Randy or Gene. There may have been fisting or a tea party. I just auto turn off the images when they start to flood my mind even if I am in a sound sleep.

What I do remember, clearly and with cold understanding, is the wakeup. I was naked in the middle of the hallway, thankfully inside the apartment. I could not see the welt of purple, gold and green forming across the bottom of my ass cheeks. The ringing of my cell phone woke me, the volume growing louder with each trill. Pushing myself up off the thick oriental carpet runner, I stumbled to the bedroom while shielding my eyes against the white hot brightness of the sun, my head throbbing.

Gene and Randy lay in a tangle across the bed. I can't bring myself to recount everything saw around the room; traces of powder, piles of powder, bottles, pipes-it looked like 1978 had exploded in the bedroom. The phone kept ringing as I squinted, realizing that I must have stripped or been stripped back in the living room so stumbled back into that vast room, barking my shin on an ottoman covered in what was either unborn harp seal or Dalmatian. The cuff of my jeans stuck out from under the footstool, and yanking them out I fished my wafer thin telephone out of a pocket.

"'Lo," was all I could manage.

"You are supposed to be leaving for the airport in less than half an hour."

Claire.

"He doesn't know you aren't in the hotel. James has been calling you all night. Your father has had a heart attack and is undergoing surgery. When James couldn't reach you, he called me. I know about the party at the house so I hope you aren't going to fuck up again. Get back to the hotel NOW. Do not miss that car to the airport!" The line went dead and I had a thousand and six thoughts freight training through my head but did not have time to consider any of the individual cars on the train as I skinned into my foul smelling clothes, grabbed my jacket and shot out of the door.

The doorman offered to call a cab but I had no time to waste, blasting out onto the street where I slammed shoulders against shoppers, dog walkers, children being nannied and was nearly taken out by an SUV size stroller as I made my way *Frogger* style across the streets and sidewalks of the city back to the hotel, arriving just in time to get my few clothes and toiletries thrown into a suitcase before the bellman arrived to take the bag. Told you I hardly ever lifted anything but weights at the Bowen gym.

Running a cold cloth over my face, I knew it would not clean up the hot adrenaline I was but better than doing nothing.

Hurrying to the elevator, I was working my arms into the now horrid smelling jacket and found a wad of bills big enough to choke, well anything brave enough to have tried to wrestle that much cash away from me. I did not remember getting to the payment portion of the evening but we must have and it seemed like I had double or triple the money Gene had promised. I shuddered, wondering what I might have done to have earned that kind of cash.

"You ok?" William Bowen asked, truly concerned about me as I got into the car.

"No," I said, with an honesty that surprised me. I managed to blink back the marble size tears welling up in my eyes as the car wove into the mid morning traffic I had just run through. The sweat from running across mid town had caught up to me by then, soaking through my jeans and t shirt. The residual drugs were still coursing through my veins as well.

"God. Rude, and you stink."

"Sorry." I sniped.

"I don't know what you did last night but I don't want to have to remind you again that you are the face of Bowen and…" Raising a hand, I cut him off mid rant. I was in the depth of physical misery, nausea and chills were settling in, and the sweat had turned to a cold clammy sheen on my skin. I'd heard the "winners train" speech and was in no mood to hear it again. As far as I knew, Bowen knew nothing of my family; it's not like we had long personal chats on those long plane rides. Even on the longest trip he would be at his computer while I was at mine, although I was usually looking at porn or playing Bejeweled. I hardly ever saw him at the office; okay, okay, I went out of my way to avoid him there. I didn't punch a time clock, true, but I also knew I had a right to a personal life.

Well sorta….wasn't I the guy waaaaayyyy back in Chapter One who was just happy to be Interviewed? I guess some familiarity was breeding some contempt. And although I had been bedded by nearly the entire client list (for all I knew), the boss himself had not hit on me at all, even had helped put me to bed and left me in my underwear not long ago.

Bet he peeked, though.

"My father is sick," was all I managed to blurt before a fist size know of emotion raced up my windpipe, cutting off the rest of my words.

The boss was silent on the rest of the ride to the airport, leaving me to close my eyes and lean my head against the seat in peace. It was truly all I could do to keep from breaking into racking sobs. Not just out of concern for my father, but for the horrible situation I had myself in by being in such bad shape.

The small plane darted down the runway (and get me, no Xanax!) and I was nearly asleep by the time we reached altitude.

The jolt woke me. The second, third and fourth froze me in fear.

At first, I thought I had slept through the flight and that we were landing, but at that split second the pilot came onto the intercom, announcing we were going down for an emergency landing and to buckle up. I already was; I had a second to glance over at William Bowen and was going to say something when the oxygen masks dropped from their (well hidden!) overhead compartments and the plane shuddered violently, then dropped.

Eleven

It's funny what you think about when you are about to die. My life did not flash before my eyes, I didn't see a tunnel of light or hear the voice of a God. I thought about food, that I had at least had a fun last meal by snacking my way across New York, and would never again need to be concerned about eating stone soup. That thought process took nanoseconds to process. The food thought was followed by me screaming though the oxygen mask, which was followed by calm as the jet suddenly smoothed out, hit a few more hard bumps, then turned downward into a long slow descent.

"This landing will be rough. Heads down and hold tight," the captain's voice came through the intercom. It was bright outside, the world rushing by the small round windows. I caught glimpses of trees, mountain side, a brilliant blue sky and suddenly we had touchdown, a screeching herky-jerky landing that bounced William Bowen and me hard against our seats. Rough? That was an understatement…along the line of the pilot of the *Hindenburg* announcing a little fire. As soon as the plane stopped bouncing over the tarmac like a demented grasshopper, Charlie, the cabin attendant, was there in a flash helping Bowen up as the pilot threw the hatchway door open and grabbed Bowen while the attendant pushed. The next thing I knew, I was again alone and sprawled on a floor, second time in less than six hours in fact for that little trick. Clearly, I was the expendable half of our duo when it came to rescue operations.

Pulling myself up, I wasted no time getting out into the cold mountain air and down the small steps to the group waiting as the lone rescue vehicle came barreling toward us. Once the very competent volunteer emergency responders were assured we were alright, we were taken back to the tiniest airport in the Rocky Mountains. The crew left with the mechanics to begin figuring out whatever the fudge had happened to cause us to go DOWN but not crash, leaving William Bowen and me alone in that smallest of airports.

Where I did impress the hell out of the boss by using the only land line I could find to call the one motel that had a room left because I didn't have a phone signal, then found what passed for a taxi service, a battered but moving 4X4 truck that delivered us to the aptly named "Dew Drop Inn." Where I got us checked into the remaining room, one bed naturally, and left William Bowen to get into a hot bath while I went to forage for food. I was, in other words, assisting the hell out of the situation.

The horrifying hangover?

Gone.

Somewhere between the PLUMMETING TOWARD THE EARTH AT THE SPEED OF FLIGHT and the connection to the pure oxygen mask and now the high, clear mountain air, I felt terrific. Of course my heart was pounding at the rate of speed equal to the rate of a humming bird flaps its wings. Despite all of that wonderful clean air, I don't think I had taken a breath since the first jolt off the plane. The fright of nearly checking off the mortal coil works wonders on a hangover. I even found myself feeling hungry!

Thankfully, the small café attached to the motel was open. Ordering a chicken takeout dinner for William Bowen, I scarfed a hamburger while waiting. Being in a near plane crash is NOT a recommended hangover cure, so I soaked up some fries with the burger just to sate off future nausea.

Back in the room, which was smaller than the plane cabin, William Bowen had finished with his bathing and come back into the room with only a towel cinched around his waist. As he stretched a white t shirt over his head, I was afforded time to gawk at his runners legs. Just because I had never seen him trotting around the grounds of Rose Bud or in the gym at the same time, it didn't mean he didn't have an exercise program. And whatever it was, it was working. I felt myself begin to thicken just being near the sexy fuck. He had towel dried that thick hair, no product was in it, which made him softer and sexier than I had ever seen him. Of course, there was just a towel between me and the Bowen rock pile, too. Sliding the tray of food onto the desk, I let that be my focus that kept me from openly staring at him.

Snagging his slacks off the bed, he slid them back up over his legs, letting the towel fall away as he expertly caught the clasps and cinched them closed, allowing me just the briefest glimpse of his stark white boxers. Why the fudge was that sexier than seeing the erect members of most of the guys he had done business with in the last few months? I got my eyes pulled away from his crotch just before he caught me. He frightened, intimidated, fascinated and turned me on all at once. Judging from Colton, however, I was not his type and Bowen was not the type to mix business with pleasure, but there was till that pull toward the unknown of doing it with the boss – which I knew was not a good idea in my situation especially – so I packed that little fantasy firmly back into my head although here we were in a nearly porn movie setting. Boss and assistant stranded for the night, sharing a bed in a cheap motel.

Well, I planned to sleep on the floor, not that I didn't trust myself but after all the floor time I had logged recently, what were a few more z's down there for me? I was pretty certain I didn't sleep walk but knowing me and my sexual record, I might very well give sleep blowjobs.

"Would it be alright if I made a call? I'll pay for it, but I still don't have reception."

"Just call," he said sternly, with a nod toward the telephone on the desk, a grin fixed so I would know it was okay.

I didn't go into detail with the brother who answered the family phone, just got the information that Dad was in pretty serious condition and would be operated on soon. Meaning I should get there pronto. The news sent the blackmail/whorish behavior of my recent life to the back burner of my mind. I loved my family fiercely but had put THEM on the back burner for too long; it shouldn't have taken this to bring them back into focus. The irony of the situation, of course, being that I couldn't get to them until the plane was repaired.

"Everything ok?" he asked when I hung up. He was still eating and had not turned around, and as I studied the long tan column of his neck I felt a twitch in my crotch again and was glad to have made the decision to sleep on the floor.

"No.   They have to operate and I need to be there."

"Of course you do," Bowen said. He turned to face me. "Been a pretty rough day, huh?" He didn't know the half of it.

"Yeah," I muttered as I sat down on the only other chair in the room, a battered overstuffed piece that should have been taken to an upholstery shop about a decade earlier and thrown out.

"Did the pilot call yet?"

"No."

The emotion of the day must have shown on my face because he smiled at me, a sincere warm gesture.

"I've been through worse," he said, leaning forward in the chair in a relaxed way I had never seen him as he began telling me about other plane mishaps and close calls. Information that did not come in a Bowen welcome packet, or I certainly would have given the flying portion of the program some deeper thought. While the stories were horrifying, they did serve as a great icebreaker for us, and he soon had me telling him about my family, the farm, my friends and soon we were talking like, well, friends. He had a true compassion about my father's health, then went on to tell me some about the Bowen family – his demanding father and distant mother. Coming out had caused a rift that never healed but he had not been kicked out of the big house and I knew people who had been thrown out of their homes like they were trash when they were in their teens, so no big boo-hoo for Bowen there. And while we were in a third rate motel in the only hick town left in Colorado, we were still in a hick town with a runway that had saved our asses and we were waiting for his private jet to be repaired. So even if he's had a few bumps along the way, his life had just gotten better.

Not complaining, though, this conversation was certainly better than some we'd had recently!

We left the room in search of a bar and found one attached to the café. Ordering a pitcher of beer, we settled in and continued our talk.

Last thing I really needed was beer on top of my recent hangover air cure, but in light of the situation I felt entitled.   And I had SO many questions that a little liquid lubricant might help with. Like how big was his cock, did he know that James did drag, did he want to fuck and most important of all, could he help me bury Colton somewhere on the estate.

But I managed to keep those to myself and stuck to family history.

By the time we had finished a pitcher and a half, the place was clearing out and our conversation had begun to be punctuated with yawns despite the excitement of the day. It was all beginning to catch up to us and for me the thrill of being this close to

Bowen, feeling like we were actually friendly for the first time, almost let me forget that we had nearly plummeted to earth like we were filled with wet cement only a few hours earlier.

A light snow had begun to fall, the romance of walking back to the motel with my very handsome employer making me long to be part of a couple again. Yeah, there were uncertainties and there had been that infidelity but still in the end to be sharing a special moment with a special someone, well it made me go all goose fleshy. I had been through some stuff alone in the last 24 hours (hadn't had time to check out the bruising on my butt or to even conjecture how it got there but knew it was probably a rainbow riot of color by then) including being high, drink, hung over, hungry and now had worked my way back to feeling both romantic and horny. Those feelings, coupled with the beer, made grabbing William Bowen's hand or sinking to my knees in the new snow and planting my face in his crotch very difficult not to do.

Back in the room we silently stripped out of our clothes. Leaving my underwear on, I moved to rummage in the closet for an extra blanket. Yanking a worn, thin piece of material off the shelf, I wrapped it around myself and snagged a pillow off the bed.

"What 'r you doing?" came from Bowen, who was already snugged down into the full size bed. It was odd hearing the always-in-control boss slur a word.

"Gonna crash over here," I managed.

"Fuck that. Get your ass in bed."

I hesitated. Bosses shouldn't be buddies. Even the ones you are hard for. But until tonight he hadn't been a buddy and this was a special set of circumstances and there was the possibility that he might bring "Winner train/losers…" into play again, so I didn't let him ask twice, just dropped the blanket (but not my inhibitions, we saw where THAT led me the night before) and slid into bed next to my boss.

We were so close that I could feel the heat radiate from his thigh and smell the combination of the cheap soap supplied by the Dew Drop Inn and beer from his breath. And the scent of his money, which was like underlying cologne, that part of his smell was honey tinged and laced with security to my nostrils.

"You know you are my best assistant ever."

"Thank you," was all I could come up with. The other "up" involved my dick, which was of course rising in salute.

"None of them could hold a candle to you. And you are so fucking cute." My now fully hard dick jumped at this. "All the clients love you…." His voice trailed off, falling to a whisper. "Wish I could have a guy like…."

Well, this was a game changer and the cat seemed to be outa the bag, huh? I didn't think he meant I was loved for my sparkling wit or dashing sense of dress. If a poll was made of the Bowen client list I'd sexed up, a man would agree that anything I wore looked its best when lying next to a bed.

He had trailed off, leaving the last unspoken words to hang over my heart. So should I make the move, wait for him?

Let's find out!

"Mr. Bowen, do you think," *we should think about this* was how I was going to finish but instead got shushed by a kiss. A sweet, tender kiss.

"Billy," he whispered while pulling his lips away gently. "Tonight call me Billy."

This did not bode well. Did that mean tomorrow was going to be back to calling him boss or Mr. Bowen? To answer my mental, unasked question from just a SHORT time ago ("*do you think…*), this was NOT a good idea, but the train seemed to have left the station as "Billy" had let his hand rove over to my thigh and it was now heading toward my crotch.

"God, you aren't only hot but you fit the suits like a glove."

Odd commentary, but I'm a guy and by then only ONE thing was on my mind as my breathing grew choppy and shallow with the distraction of his strong fingers approaching crotch central in my world. Hard and ready, as noted, it didn't matter what I thought and felt about what was about to happen, because I'm a guy and that is the way we roll. The sex bus just doesn't stop once it is in gear.

Usually.

Just as his fingers grazed my balls his phone jangled to life, the Calvary in the form of a ringtone. I may not have had bars, but William Bowen certainly did. I suspected he had a plan so complete he could reach NASA, the President, or Martha Stewart any time he wanted.

I understood why he changed the course of his fingers from me to the phone, but still was a little let down. As YOU well know, I'd been pining for a piece of him since the interview and this might have been our only chance if I were on the chopping block. Despite his kind words of such a short time ago, I'd been lied to before ("NO, I'm NOT having an affair!" could have been the title of a two act play by the former love of my life), so now kinda expected it.

From what I was overhearing (and I was close to the hot fucker, close enough to still be ROCK hard and ready), the call was about the plane and the news not good.

"How long to get the parts?"

"Do we still have full power?"

"I have to be in Colorado Springs by two PM."

Question, question, statement, hang up. Classic William Bowen.

"Sorry, Wyatt. The repair is going to take several days and I have that meeting. The plane has full power and the internet is up, so I need you to get back there, figure out how to get me to Colorado Springs and you home."

Sliding out of bed, keeping myself as turned as possible away from Bowen with my hard on pushing out the front of my underwear, I wrapped myself back in my stinky clothes and hurried out the door before I could let my fantasies about William Bowen overtake me and crawl back under the bed covers with him.

Trudging through the now deeper snow toward the office, the light romantic flakes falling earlier had given way to big wet quarter size chunks that were being driven by an increasing wind. Would I get home in time to see my father if he took a turn for the worse? Would Bowen remember what had almost happened and would it change things between us? I had a lot on my mind to keep me from thinking of the horrible weather I was slushing through.

I tipped the night clerk heavily from the WAD of money that had made its way into my jacket (hoping there was not a video that had gone viral showing the world what I had done to earn THAT kind of dough) and he got me to the hanger, where I poured myself a drink and took it into the tiny shower on the plane, sipping the warming beverage while standing under the rush of hot water and letting the events of the last few hours marinate.

Woke naked on the floor of a strangers apartment with serious money in my pocket, almost missed the plane, fought with Bowen, heard the news of my father's heart attack, almost had sex with the boss, almost crashed. Lotta almost for one day. I spent a long time getting arrangements made, then passed out on the small sofa in the main compartment of the plane.

By Seven PM the next evening I was, well yeah, I was still a little hung over too, but also at my father's bedside. James had met the plane I chartered to get Bowen out with a suitcase for me. I went right to PDX, the main Portland airport, and caught a commuter to the town nearest the farm. From there, I taxied to the bus terminal, bussing on into the tiny hamlet I had grown up nearest to. From there, I was picked up by one of my brothers, who wasted no time commenting on my haggard condition, who took me directly to Dad.

Mom, sister and brothers, in-laws, all had commentary and snarked about the lack of attention I had paid the family, how long it took me to get there in this time of emergency, my haircut, clothes, well just everything about me was wrong.

And I thought James and his drag buddies could be vicious.

I was resettled back into my old room, then bundled the clothes that had seen me through the streets of New York to a hustler bar to some kind of orgy to a near plane crash to near sex with the boss, a snow storm and to my father's hospital bed. The clothing needed to be retired rather than cleaned.

Crawling between the Martha Stewart K-Mart collection sheets of my childhood bed was like the hug I needed right then, being alone between them felt better than any of the expensive high thread count sheets I had been parking my carcass between in the last few months with clients.

In fresh underwear, finally, I passed out early and the next morning found out the hard way why you should never let a drag queen pack for you.

James knew I was from rural America and that there was a farm involved, but clearly had an Eva Gabor in *Green Acres* understanding of where I was going. Among my clothing choices he had packed a pair of tweed Hugo Boss slacks, an Armani turtle neck sweater and a selection of my (cute!) D&G and H&M undies. This was The Sticks, Oregon. Pendleton is our state designer and all I had to wear were high end threads. I knew the jeering I was going to take from the assorted family gathering in the kitchen for breakfast followed by caravanning to the hospital, so finally gave up trying to put a costume together from what James had sent and opened the closet door, rummaging until I found a suitable pair of jeans and a plaid shirt to wear.

I was preening in the mirror, feeling presentable to my family or ready to hit any gay Country & Western bar, and was about to follow the smells coming from below to a farm breakfast when my phone blew up.

"What the FUCK happened in New York!"

TWELVE

No hi, how are you, how is your father-nothing but raw energy and emotion from James.

"Huh?" was my snappy and well thought out response.

"Claire just called and said there are some serious thuggy guys in the waiting room at Bowen looking for you."

I'd turned my telephone off when I didn't have a signal in the mountains. Pulling it away from my ear, I punched in the message button. Twenty-two since the call from Claire that woke me sprawled in the middle of Gene's hallway.

"I have no idea what you are talking about." Well, there was some immediate suspicion that something had gone wrong based on the wad of money in my jacket pocket. My eyes shifted to my bundle of dirty clothing.

"These guys are serious about something but aren't coughing up a lot of detail other than you being involved in some shenanigans. Tell me what happened in New York."

"My father is about to have surgery," I intoned.

"Just tell me, man, it's for your own good," James intoned back.

I did not like the edge in his voice; it was enough to have been flayed (and kissed on a little) by Bowen, but I was not going to take snark from James. But I did give him a bare bones version of what had happened in New York, leaving out discussions of car loan size payments.

"I haven't done anything wrong!" I snarled back in self defense, although to be honest the jury was SO still out on that one.

"Sure about that?"

Well, no, but I wasn't going to let HIM know.

"They told Claire a bunch of money and some jewelry is missing from some church big shot muck. The story they told Claire, which Bowen had not heard yet, is that you and your pal set up a trick and took a few mementos. Because of his church ranking they have assured her that this guy does not want the story to get out to the press but he sure as shit wants his stuff back."

"He wasn't a trick," I lied evenly through grit teeth, wondering how the fudge I had not managed to get a pair of hit priests on my tail.

"Ok, whatever, but this could be the end of you here at Bowen."

"You can say as many mean things as you like and it doesn't scare me." I'd seen James in full face, so had no fear. "I've got more going on than you can imagine right now. You need me to help you with the bar, so help me now, man."

There was a pause, as threatening James thought my words over, then became considerate James.

"You are right. I don't know the whole story but if we don't fix this fast you are going to be on the streets and Bowen will make me his whipping boy. If it is one thing Bowen won't tolerate, it is press; it's his wicked witch. Claire wants me to come get that stuff pronto."

This was NOT going well and someone was pounding on my door.

"I don't know what the fuck you are talking about but I need to know and right now I have to go."

"Let me get some more details. Stay right there. I can get the address from Claire, right?"

"I never gave this address; only my ex has it."

"Great, he had a car, right?"

I hated bringing Mary-Kate and Ashley into this.

"Yeah, but…"

"Perfect. That way my car is here and no one knows I am gone," James was musing to himself. This is serious, Wyatt. At least as far as you and I are concerned. I'll have Claire stall the thugs and I'll call when we are on the way. How far south are you again?"

"Nearly Palm Springs," I said. "You won't be here until tomorrow and I am going to be in and out of the hosp...," I trailed off when I realized I was speaking into a dead phone. They would have to make it without my help. Shuddering, I couldn't imagine the three of them making it to the city limits of Portland sign, but I had bigger fish to fry. The knocking at my door stopped and my sister barged in, scolding me that breakfast was on and waiting for me.

Shooing her away, I grabbed my filthy bundle of clothes and plunged my fingers into my jacket and fishing out the wad of cash. Digging deeper, I excavated two thin gold rings, a magnificent gold crucifix on a hair thin gold chain, followed by a huge ring made of heavy worked gold with a ruby in the middle. I didn't need a jeweler's loupe to know the pieces were old and real.

Rifling the bills, I saw that they all looked to be hundreds. A LOT of hundreds. I didn't have time for this and kicked myself for putting myself in this situation. Holding the loot between my hands, I could see why it was wanted back. Randy had obviously set me up to be his mule to get the stuff out of the apartment.

Cramming everything back into my jacket, I hid the whole ball of mess clothing under my blankets.

After THAT start, the day was long and exhausting. There were complications but Dad came through, everyone got to see him in recovery and for the time I was with my family, with Portland, Bowen, Randy, New York, near plane crashes and even the terror twins out of my mind.

Hours later, finally snugged back into my bed getting the first sound sleep I'd had in months and oblivious to the world with exhaustion, my phone rang. I tried to ignore it, but knew I had to pick up. The alarm next to my bed read four-thirty seven AM. James and the boys had made it to the village and wanted me to come meet them. I explained that the nightlife gene we had all grown since leaving our homes and merging into the city did not work here. There were no 24 hour diners or coffee shops. No clubs, cafes, dens of iniquity or even grocery stores would be open yet. They had to sullenly accept directions to a chain restaurant by the freeway where I hurried to meet them. I didn't need the three of them coming into the century plus old farm house like a gay pride parade – no shame in that game but the family had limits.

I was exhausted and had fallen right to sleep. The only reason I had not swallowed half a dozen Xanax was that my bottle was empty.

"Good God, what part of Dogpatch is this!" James sighed as he sank into the booth across from me, Thing One snugging in next to him while the ex scrunched in next to me.

"You look good in this," the ex Mr. Me purred while plucking at the material, the former best friend nodding in agreement. I ignored the compliments as I figured the pair was probably just smelling the money and jewelry.

"What the fuck is going on?" I demanded as the waitress came around with the coffee pot. She poured a round and we all waited until she finished before speaking again.

"Thank you," we said like a flock of parrots. May have been on the losing end of a lot of stuff but we were keeping our manners.

"You have to listen to the entire story before saying anything. Promise." James was giving me a deadly stare. "I mean it; I'm not going to talk unless you promise."

I was pissed, tired, scared, angry and a whole lot of other stuff which was not going to resolve unless I had some concrete information, so I nodded my head slightly.

"Nope, a verbal and they are witness," nodding toward the Winklevoss twins at the table with us.

"Promise," I managed through clenched teeth in a steely tone. "Talk."

"You are, I hope, familiar with the story of Icarus. His father fashioned wings out of wax and feathers for him and Icarus so they could fly from Crete. Before they launched in flight, his father warned him not to fly too close to the sun or the sea."

"What the fu….," I started, only to be shushed into silence by the exes. James just stopped and stared until I held my end of the bargain and shut up again.

"In his flight, Icarus felt so free that he of course got farther and farther from the earth and neared the sun, which melted the wax and he plunged back into the sea and drowned." He took a sip of coffee. "There is more to the story involving a labyrinth and a minotaur and the underworld in general but we don't need any of that right now. We'll just bookmark that there and get back to it anyway. William Bowen was not always the savvy businessman you know. He inherited Bowen but a board of directors really runs the show. And they make Bowen look like a kindly maiden aunt. The Bowen family has run Portland since settling in. There isn't a politician on either side of the house they do not influence. Well, Bill doesn't influence because he is the last one.

The waitress arrived and was waved away.

"Billy was not an ideal child; he was sewing wild oats from the beginning. William Senior liked 'em as wild as Billy but at least he married in the party line. But he didn't love her; she was a suitable sorority sister who drank. There were maids and nannies for young William while his mother went to the club and daddy ran the state as his daddy and his daddy and on and on had."

The waitress arrived again and we could not turn her away this time so we ordered and accepted refills.

"So William learned early on how to get his way. Booze, drugs and boys all came to Rose Bud early. As did the trouble." This was said in a low tone that caused us all to lean in a little bit.

"His records of course were sealed but are extensive; drunk driving, underage drinking of course, carrying a handgun without a license. Couple of rape charges that quietly went away. Guys."

There were looks all around the table at each other.

"He got shipped to one of those teen challenge places in the desert in Arizona where things got worse. Not one but two attempted murder charges there. As much money as the Bowen's had, a whole bunch of it just went right back out the door to protect that name. It was another time, the seventies and eighties, so they got stuff covered up that today would never be possible. The kind of stuff that would have made Bowen look bad. They had always been press shy but that took it to a whole new level.

Food was delivered as James continued with his oration; we did not stop him as the waitress made delivery this time. Conversation bubbled around us but the clacking of forks against plate ware was all to be heard from out table aside from James' low tone.

"How did you find all of this out?" I finally injected as he bit into a crusty English muffin.

"I've been piecing stuff together for a long while. And I have some friends at the courthouse and Claire knows everything. Now, no more questions."

I shut up reluctantly.

"The family money not only bailed Billy out but got him a pseudo business degree and his father installed him in the office. The guys he was bringing home for dinner then made Colton look like the good one. Which did not please the senior Bowens. Mrs. Bowen died followed by Mr. B.'s massive heart attack." James took another breath but no one spoke. It was hard to imagine proper, stern William Bowen as a party boy.

"The will isn't public but I found enough documents to prove that William Senior had a board of directors with enough voting power in place to keep Bill in check long before his death. Which did not sit well will Billy, needless to say. He has been funded enough to have a good life even if he never works, but he wanted the control and refused to be controlled.

Plates were cleared, and more refills given as James went on.

"But his lifestyle was pretty high so Bill started his own business off shoot from Bowen. Drugs. Major, major dealing. Well, he didn't so much fund the deals. He had that office at Bowen and if he'd just gone there and whacked off or shot up and kept to himself he would have just gone rolling merrily along but there were busts and his name started hitting the streets. Heck, even I remember hearing about him in the clubs when I was coming up and out."

"Once he got narked, the Board yanked a knot in his ass but it didn't stop him from fighting back. He lawyered up and tried to get them booted from Bowen. Which didn't work, of course, and certainly didn't endear the board to him. They have a stalemate which will never be resolved."

The breakfast crowd had filtered out; the table had been wiped again. Coffee was topped off but I was not leaving until I knew what all of this had to do with ME even if we had to go into luncheon overtime.

"But all of that is not where we are now," James sighed, while draining another cup of coffee. "I've been with Bowen about five years, seen the bad boys he has drug into the house, but have never seen any drugs. Trust me, I've looked. Oh, some of his tricks and temporary house pets have brought in some pot and a little blow but nothing more than I have seen," he assured the fascinated trio of Dixie, Pixie and me who crowded the table.

"Claire took me to the office." With that he reached into his jacket and pulled out an envelope and tossed it to me. I lifted the flap and found pictures of hot men in compromising positions with men I knew. Cal Harper, Lew Frazier, Tom Overbay among them. And Mattey.

For every photo there was a connecting picture of a young guy in a suit, one of MY suits, and the guys all looked, well, like me. Same studio shot, same suit; we looked enough alike that we could have been Xeroxed.

"What the fuck…'" I trailed off while grabbing pictures back out of the hands of the exes.

"Seems Bowen found a way to keep his revenue stream up while not having to do a lot of up selling to keep the board off his back."

At the bottom of the stack were shots of me, with all of the above and in stripper like poses in all of those executive bathrooms. Those big mirrors were two way and had covered camera lenses. Since these clear as a bell stills showing my every freckle were taken frame by frame, I knew there were videos as well.

"He flew too close to the sun by whoring out his assistant, his best and favorite, from all accounts." I murmured as much to the table at large as to myself; shame, horrible, horrible shame wracking me. Not from the fact that I was facing the music of me, but that I had actually thought after that near night in the motel that Bowen might really HAVE liked me as James said. I wanted to cry-die-scream-none of those emotions were helped by the fact that this was all being shared with the man who had broken my heart and the man who had betrayed me as a best friend.

I could only guess that Bowen got the other guys involved and given out as the bonus the same way he did, by letting them swim deeper and deeper into the river of self denial until they drowned, like I was going down for the third time here.

Bowen may have pimped me out, but I had whored myself out.

"How much of this did you know when we talked the other day?"

"Quite a bit," James said honestly. "I couldn't imagine that you didn't know something was up, though."

"WHY didn't you say anything THEN!"

"Hey, don't get mad at me, everyone but these two has some blame here!" Scowling at me, James held a hand up, ticking his fingers closed with each point.

"Bowen is THE culprit, I just didn't tell you some stuff I assumed a smart guy like you would already know. Claire made certain the guys looked like what the Bowen clients wanted and fit the suits so he didn't have to buy new sizes in clothes, and Claire's brother the bartender gave her YOUR name because he had seen one of your pornos. So there is enough fault to be passed around, buddy. I'm here 'cause I like you and wanted to give you a heads up before some bad shit happened."

I was startled and wanted to lash out, but now didn't quite trust that James was still telling the whole tale. And he had just succeeded in making the Katzenjammer Kidz sitting at the table with us look like the GOOD guys in this story.

"Well, why rock the boat and tell me all of this now?"

"Because those thugs scared Claire. I was going to tell you after I'd made the bar proposition to Bowen."

"So what happened?"

"Bowen monitors every call made on a Bowen phone," well that explained a lot, "and knew you were meeting that kid Randy and where. It turned out that Bowen also happened to know that the guy Randy was tricking with was in charge of some major contracts with the church Bowen wanted. So he let you go; you were kind of the gift with purchase."

I felt dirty and used and wanted to have my soul dry cleaned but was not giving up a penny of that hard (on) earned cash.

"So when cash and jewelry turned up missing, the guy had Randy tracked down, and he pointed the finger at you."

I just couldn't speak.

"The thuggy guys were throwing threats around that made it clear their guy in New York isn't happy about this, threats like he was taking this to the board and the cops. She got them calmed down by assuring they would get the jewelry and money back but anything can still happen. It's a stupid threat because the cops would want information on Randy, which is very easy to come by, but I think he was going to use the theft as leverage to try and get a better contract out of Bowen-a kind of reverse sting in his favor."

Again, and I thought Drag Queens were vicious.

Bowen had made it so easy for me and I really did know what had been going on, but turned a blind eye. While kinda falling in love with my boss I was making good money and keeping HIM in good money.

"The whole outraged thing in Rome wasn't really about me sleeping with Mattey, just that I didn't sleep with Cal, right then." The restaurant had cleared out of the breakfast crowd by then.

"Yes, Claire likes you, man, and she has felt bad that you were doing this. None of the others lasted or were even pretend good assistants and she hated seeing you used like that. And Mattey wasn't beaten. He just told you that to be mean. He had someone from housekeeping go back into the room and get your stuff so he could return it."

Even being told that Mattey was not harmed and that Claire liked me couldn't bring up my mood.

"All the spilled milk and juice at the start," I whispered.

"Dribble glasses; some of 'em wanted to see the new meat before even talking to Bowen about contracts.

I wanted to crawl in a hole and to, to, to….fuck.

Well, it was all over but the shouting for now.

"Sorry, James, you are going to have to get the bar on your own. I'm out of Bowen."

"I'm not thinking about that man," he responded defensively. To his credit, he sounded sincere.

"I'll take this stuff back to her myself," I said, as we finally rose to leave. I called my family and told them I had to go back to Seattle and there was much unhappiness despite my assuring them I would be right back.

And I was, just not under quite the circumstances I had been expecting.

THIRTEEN

I liked the still shot CNN was using of me, but was not at all happy with the (heavily) edited porn movie clips of me some of the local channels were using. Channel 2 was using only the Bowen corporate shot of me, which I was quite fond of. The suit made me look so, well, corporate, but we have already discussed how well fitted they were.

Every few weeks, in fact, a new suit had arrived in the Bowen offices from the Italian tailor. Shoes, belts, ties and shirts included. The underwear that arrived in these clothing care packages was from an American concern, however. Skimpy and tight usually, but the occasional pair of boxer or boxer briefs thrown in. I got to send everything including the undies to the corporate account for dry cleaning. Bowen wanted me dressed nice, which I always was until the client or I undressed me at the end of the day, or meeting as it were. You WOULD think I would have thought something of that but I was too busy with the suits and sex and money and, well, everything but what Bowen Industries did. Candle dipping, chocolate molding, stuffed animal manufacture? Still didn't know, wasn't pushing hard to know but now that I did know, on what part of my operation was I actually going to pull the plug?

But by the time our merry little band made its way out of the backwater where a good chunk of my naïve life had taken place and up I-5 to Portland, the plug on my future had not only been pulled, but neatly severed.

Techno music blasting (we were in gay-boi pack mode, what can I say), we went right to Bowen, parking in my spot in the garage because I had left my car at the apartment. Tired but hydrated and gummed up – it was amazing how many stops for liquid and chewable items we had to make for Dora and his Explorer. Eerily, they hadn't asked for potty breaks as well.

Storming into the office, I was ready to start my beheadings with Claire. She was running a shredder, her bartender brother who had turned me on to her handing her documents. Before I could say a word, she pointed to the flat screen television on the dark paneled wall opposite her desk where I saw the first images of myself being played. Before I could wrap my head around that, she stood and moved into my little corner office and grabbed the remote for the flat screen mounted on what was soon to no longer by my wall and flicked it on as the ex twins and James crowded in. The exes had never been in my office so there was a lot of head swiveling on their part while the sight of me on TV kept James, Claire, Jody and I captivated. It was a local affiliate playing a feed from a national network:

"….*Bowen Industries, headquartered in Portland. The scandal is rocking the financial world from here to the heartland* (a shot of Indianapolis flashed on the screen), *to southern California, South Florida,* (a shot of Cal and me came to the screen, WHAT THE FUCK!), *New York, Washington D.C. and internationally to Rome….*"

Images of me and men from all of the places flooded the screen, mixed with more images from my porn career.

Sheesh.

Claire, cold, efficient scary Claire – the woman I wanted to Friend me on Facebook more than any other, gave a sigh, then leaned forward and hugged me. I couldn't very well hate her now, especially for doing her job just like I had been doing my job.

"Colton knows Randy, found out what happened in New York, and hit LA with the story for sale," she said with a grimace. "We," she said with a nod toward a sheepish but still very cute Jody, "are cleaning things up here. Bowen has a team of attorneys working on this so get out of here and do not let anyone know where you are. NO ONE."

"You," she was now pointing at James, "take him back to where you found him and leave him there, then get your ass back to Rose Bud. You two, her steady gaze moved to Kermit and Miss Piggy, never saw him. Open a mouth, sell a story and bad stuff will happen. Bad."

"I'm quitting," I started.

"Quit now and you are on your own. Do you have what you need to leave with me or do I need to take it from you?" And she was MY friend I'd just found. I hoped Cheng and Eng were paying attention because she meant business. I handed over the money and jewelry while staring at the screen where another image of me wrapped around yet another male torso was being displayed.

"What's going on?" I managed. "And why were the other guys here for the interview if you all knew I was the chosen one?"

"It had to LOOK like he was open to hiring anyone. Al Capone was taken down by the IRS for Christ sake, now GO! And NO ONE has seen you, got it?" The group didn't even need to nod. "Now get out of here; you were never here today. YOU, the pointing was back at me, no calls, texts, emails, smoke signals. We will find you if we need to. Until then, do not talk to anyone. You open your mouth even one time and you are on your own. And for God's sake cover him up when you leave the garage." Like a startled group of antelope, the little group turned as one and fled the office. I didn't have time to even ask for a refill of my pills.

"Wyatt," Claire called as I was in the elevator car. Reaching out, I broke the Eye beam with my hand which held the doors apart. "I'm sorry, really. I shouldn't have let this happen."

That was NOT the way I had planned to be leaving the Bowen corporate office. I'd come in as innocent as Elly Mae Clampett but had learned a few things and was going to storm Bowen's office as Faye Dunaway as Joan Crawford in *Mommy Dearest*; *Don't fuck with me fellas, this ain't my first time at the rodeo....*

My demands were going to be simple and straightforward, to be on the payroll until I found another job and to have insurance until I had another job. I figured I had made Bowen enough to get that at least. I had my little nest egg of dirty money (well it was) but he didn't need to know about that. But he probably already DID know about that, in fact my anger had grown when I realized that he must have been behind suggesting that the clients tip me and that he hadn't made it a higher number. I was going to tell him I was going to send the suits, shoes and accessories I had at the apartment. I did not plan to tell him I was keeping the cute underwear.

But I was denied even that and now more angry at myself than anything else. More importantly, I was upset that I had DONE NOTHING WRONG. Bowen really hadn't either, for that matter. It's not

TAILOR MADE

like he asked me to have sex with anyone or told me to; those choices had been mine and on my own time but most of those facts were being overlooked and ignored by the press.

"It's okay, Claire, we all make mistakes," I managed in a very humane way I must say, given the circumstances, but I did feel like she and I were even for the calls saving my ass a time or three. And I still felt that under different circumstances she and I could have been great girlfriends but that was not in the stars. Dropping my hand, I let the elevator doors close.

Back in the garage, we crowded back in the junk food wrapper and hair product (gay boys travel with the most essential stuff; combs, mousse, jel, sprays and enough diet Coke cups to fill a silo) filled seats. I sat shotgun, head spinning. James was driving again; Lucy and Ethyl were the rear guard and had just started exclaiming over my office and the Bowen tower in general when I heard;

"Get him down!"

Never played ball so am not familiar with the term "heads up" but the tone in James voice told me to respond so down I went, one of the two in the back throwing a Hugo Boss sweater over me as I hit the floorboard. I felt the car lurch and we shot out of the garage like we were on fire.

"What the FUCK!" I needed information NOW. The radio was snapped on, dial scanned. I started to lift my head only to have it slammed back down.

"Stay there!"

"More breaking news on the scandal at Bowen Industries," a radio announcer intoned, a current of joy in his voice. And that is how we learned the rest of the story. Which made my little blackmail situation with Colton look like a prank.

I will never understand all of the details of what became the Bowen Scandal, but while Bill Junior had been at the helm he had taken the family business to some deep dark places. Which had been easy to do because Bowen, it turned out, was a pretty big pie made up of a lot of different berries as their portfolio. Finance, manufacture, trade, all set against a back drop of politics. There wasn't a political name in the state in ANY party that was not being linked and the biggest issue of all was that despite what was going on I had done nothing wrong.

Well, perhaps that part of the story was the most important to me.

Bowen, who had been involved with all of these people for decades, was going down not because of anything illegal, but because of the immorality of Bill Junior as he was being called by the media, who had not forced me into prostitution but had certainly led me to it, while his hands were laying the ground work for my shenanigans. Dorothy Parker had it dead on for us when she said, *"You can lead a whore to water but you can't make her think."* I had certainly not been doing much thinking while enjoying the many perks and very little work responsibility expected of me at Bowen Industries.

James dropped Hansel and Gretel at the apartment and hit the gas, finally letting me up off the floor somewhere outside the city limits sign. When he finally stopped for a lunch of fast food next to a freeway off ramp, he told me about the crowd of paparazzi waiting outside of Bowen – they appeared as quickly as the scandal had broken. Back on the road we listened in mounting horror to the details of the story. The size of my penis was mentioned at least three times by one host. Didn't expect THAT when I woke up and was dreading the reaction of my family, but I had nowhere else to go.

The story of William Bowen and his ASS-istant was THE news of the day. Colton had killed the goose and his sound bites were all over the radio so I knew he was on television as well. Every man who had done business with Bowen was ducking, covering and screaming that they were married, church going family men who had never done anything wrong. Colton had managed to get his long blond fingers on photos, however, and once they were released a whole lotta guys were coming up with NEW stories as to why they were being shown with me in those compromising positions. Oh, the radio play we listened to, my name coming up every third line or so, was more exciting than that Orson Wells October 30, 1938 broadcast of *War of the Worlds* about aliens landing on earth. I could not even begin to imagine what WAS happening on television, in fact, and could not help but hope we would make it home in time for me to hear my name come out of the mouth of Mary Hart.

The upshot of everything was that I was the last of a series of whores Bowen had been using to seal international deals, tale (and, well, tail,) as old as time. The difference being that I had willingly slept with these guys and that was a fact that was not making it into ANYONE'S version of the story. I mean from a journalistic POV, why would you include that? No story there, move along now! But the big businessman who is willing to hire not only the guy of his client dreams but that the same guy is willing to sleep with the clients to get the contract for the boss, well there you have journalistic gold! We, William Bowen and I, were making the Teapot Dome Scandal, Watergate, the Clinton Affair and the Birther Controversy all seem pretty tame. The true story would have been so boring; covering that would have made me just another gay tramp on the street.

I was SO glad I had not fallen in love with that rat bastard Bowen. So glad his thick chestnut brown hair and twinkly blue eyes still didn't make me swoon from time to time, that his overpowering sexiness didn't still give me chills when we sat near each other on that spiffy little jet, that his laugh didn't excite me, the temptation of being so close to him in bed, feeling the heat of his skin and wanting to reach over and stroke my hands over his broad chest and thick biceps, so glad his electric smile hadn't made me tingle the few times he used it on me. I was NOT in love with the boss who had just spent months abusing my trust.

There, I said it.

Well, to myself at least.

Luckily, I WAS so mad at him right then I couldn't see straight and didn't care if I ever saw him again.

On top of what the hot and rich William Bowen hadn't done (but had allowed me to do to myself), I was pissed that he was making me for the first time ever happy to paraphrase the opening line of a favorite movie, *Out of Africa,* that *"I had a fah-m...,"* to run to even if it was only waaayyy to the south of Salem and not in Africa.

FOURTEEN

"...I felt nothing and Carp allowed it, which really made me burn. They were so helpful, they called me hopeless but I really didn't know where else to turn. Six months later I heard that Carp had died so I dug right down to the bottom of my soul and cried...,'cause I felt nothing...."

Another of those songs from *A Chorus Line* was running through my head again. Should have been paying royalties for the use of that show as often as I had the lyrics running through my brain. But that was pretty much how I was feeling...numb and nothing. I was keeping emotion at bay as details of the scandal rolled in, flooding local and national news like I was Monica Lewinsky, Fidel Castro and several Kardashians all rolled into one.

If I'd managed to keep the cash portion of even a tiny chunk of any of those porn movies, I would have been making bank while doing farm chores, but nope, didn't think of that while my DVDs were flying off the shelves and being discreetly shipped worldwide in discreet brown paper wrappers and streaming to computers on probably an interplanetary basis right then. I was the most popular cock on the block, no doubt, but you would never have known it if you had seen me dressed in jeans and a t shirt being chased by the small herd of goats I was trying to keep fed or scattering grain for the chickens or any number of other farm chores I had been charged with.

Considering my father's surgery and what was going on, my family was taking this well. Well, as well as this kind of thing COULD be taken. James dropped me at the gate (yes, the fucking GATE) of the lane leading to the house, leaving me to scan the ground on my walk of shame home for good soup size rocks because I now knew what was in my past but the future was still an unwritten book.

There were quiet faces trained on the television screen in the old farm house, but thankfully no one asked a lot of questions and the news was doing a pretty good job of filling them in on the sordid details and I wasn't offering any information although I HAD DONE NOTHING WRONG!

After that, the hours turned into days, days into weeks and my anger grew at Bowen until I wouldn't have fucked him with anyone else's dick, let alone with my own. To top that off, I heard nothing from anyone: Bowen, James, Claire, Jody – I would have been happy with a "Hey" text from Jean or the stone faced driver by then. The only news I was getting all came from, well, the news. On the upside, the press had not found me, so I was not being hounded. James, Bowen, Claire, Jean, Stone Face and Jody HAD all been featured in clip after clip on the news, however, along with the men who had slept with me along the line.

The scandal did start to simmer down; I assume sales of my DVDs slowed. Bowen was removed from the board, contracts were nullified, careers ruined, families shattered. I could only hope some of them could repair themselves with honesty and live happier lives and that their families would not suffer too much. If everyone could be open and accepting of who they are and what they want in the first place things like this wouldn't have happened, but they always had and probably always would, sadly. Hey, they asked to sleep with me, okay? I wasn't connected with, holed up with or involved with anyone who wasn't already on my side of the tramp pasture – and I was out, single and open!

About three weeks back on the farm, my father home and healing, the family had scattered and life moved on at its usual pace. I was out on the tractor of mine turning ground late one afternoon when over the muffled noise of the motor I heard an even louder noise.

At first I thought it was an earthquake since I was blasting techno on my headphones, then saw the helicopter approaching. It started as a black dot, moving closer and closer until settling onto the middle of the field I was working on. This was it, I figured, the press had found me. At least I looked hot as blazes; the farm work had been better for me than my routine at the Bowen gym. Shirtless and in tight jeans and boots, battered cowboy hat cocked on the back of my head, my smooth chest was streaked with sweat, my eyes were protected by vintage aviator shades from the late 1970's. I may have been hating on where I was and what I was doing, but I looked damn hot doing it.

But it wasn't Billy Bush or Katie Couric or even Mario Lopez who came out of the small craft.

It was William Bowen, looking sexy as ever in his own jeans and crisp white shirt. I had stopped the tractor and had to smile as I saw him stumble over a freshly turned furrow while lifting an arm to wave at me. How he had found me was a puzzle. Had he tagged me during that night of nearly naked dancing at Rose Bud?

But that puzzle didn't stretch out long. As I popped the ear pieces from my head, I realized he found me through the phone. The phone I was playing music on was also the Bowen paid phone he had always been able to reach me on and now realized he (well, someone he paid) tracked my every move with. Think me arrogant and self centered for that? Perhaps, but I was a Bowen property just like a file cabinet I now knew.

I sat still, letting him come to me. Bowen made it to the tractor. The wash from the still rotating blades had mussed his hair up sexily. He looked up offering a half smile, and I wanted to run him down with the tractor for even having the thought that he was still hot."

"Did you know about the porn?"

No "Hi", "Hey", "Hello." I hit him with the question that had been gnawing at me rather than with the tractor.

"Of course." He figured the first honest thing he said to me was going to be that truth. "Bowen does extensive background checks." He didn't even look ashamed about what had happened.

"Do you have a moral compass?" Still perched on the tractor seat. "Why didn't you just hire hookers or send escorts with bows on to the clients."

"They are family men for the most part and needed to be safe."

My mind was on fire.

"And I was the tested gift with purchase!"

"Is there someplace we can talk?"

Ha. Advantage me. And I hoped I was driving him crazy with my shirtless body.

"I'm only on your payroll until this is over, and when is that by the way?" I was furious.

"I have some things to say to you."

"And I have a word or two for you as well."

"Look, I started out doing one thing but it changed. Yes I'd seen the DVDs and I knew you'd fit the suits and that you were the kind of guy my clients liked. You have to admit it was profitable for all of us," Bowen said, smile back in place.

"How did you know," I asked, anger starting to burn in my stomach again, "I'd go along with what you needed me to do?" Using the thumb of my leather glove covered right hand, I reached up and tipped the worn hat back.

"Didn't," he said with a shrug, "but once I saw you stripped down at Lew's, I knew you were what the guys were looking for."

I was silent.

"You watched….,"

"Wyatt, I've made mistakes. I never meant for any of this to happen."

I cut him off again. "You sure as fuck did." Seething, I started the tractor again.

"I've been taken off the board and I came to apologize."

Shutting the tractor off again, I jumped off of it, landing with a whumph of dust in a furrow in front of Bowen.

"You used me as a corporate gift, got me hooked on pills, have had my name drug through the press from the <u>Miami Sun</u> to the <u>Nome Nugget</u>, and you just have I'm sorry to say?"

"I told you I wanted to talk," he reasoned. I suspected that in addition to the faux business degree he held that he held some kind of faux law degree as well. "Look, you are still on the payroll," implying that might come to an end at any time, "we both made some money so please listen to me, what was the harm in the end?"

William Bowen stood stock still under the hot mid day sun, a puzzled look on his face.

"What was the harm?" I said calmly instead of screaming, "you lied to me, used me and I started falling in love with you – that, William Bowen, is the harm. You had life handed to you on a silver platter while I've worked for every nickel. I may have done porn but at least it was honest work for an honest dollar. Unlike you with your fancy office and fancy degree but couldn't do business well enough to sell anything, so you sold a line of guys like me and were too cheap to even buy new suits for each guy!" Oh, I was not happy. "Now GO." Raising my arm, I pointed to the sleek little black helicopter behind us, top rotor blade still twisting lazily.

"You like me?" he asked, in a tone so low I could almost not tell what he had said. My arm was aching, that's how hard I was pointing at his little flying machine. Bowen took a step forward. He was close enough that I could smell his familiar scent. I wanted to be turned on but held back this time.

"Look, Wyatt, I've been an ass and done horrible shit." William took another step toward me. "But I really am sorry. In the last few months I've watched you like I've never watched an assistant. Well, like I've never watched another guy actually. I realized I had been wasting my time on losers. You are the first decent guy I've ever spent time with and I think I love you, too."

Well, fuck. Mr. Ex Boss waits until NOW to throw that at me. Of course I had just thrown it at him.

I thought the helicopter had stunned me, but this was a hook out of left field and I truly felt punched in the stomach.

My teeth came unhinged, my jaw popped. Bending at the waist, I drew in a fast breath and swept to one knee, my knees skidding a groove into the soft dirt as I swept a hand into the freshly plowed earth and straightened up.

A lot had happened since leaving the farm; finding love, breaking up, employment, unemployment; friends who were drag queens, and lots of cute underwear had passed my way. Travel to places far more exotic than Salem and Seattle and finding out the hard way I'd been used as an international hooker.

My fingers had scooped up a good sized dirt clod. William Bowen and I still stood staring at each other.

Feeling tears begin to sting my eyes, I pulled my hand back and launched the dirt at Bowen, who was more startled than scared. The piece of dirt smacked his stark white shirt, a dark blot of stain spreading as a confused look crossed his face. The tears started down my face openly as I leaned down and scooped up another and another and another clump of dirt, throwing, throwing, throwing until Bowen turned and finally broke into a trot back to the helicopter.

FIFTEEN

Heavy machinery and tears don't mix, so I stood there in the middle of the field letting the tears of violent, violent anger track down my cheeks while watching the helicopter become a black dot in the distance again.

I couldn't have just crushed on some random hottie straight guy or a psycho killer or someone with a wild leather fetish like I was some NORMAL gay guy. But then, I was the one who didn't go to a real job counselor or employment agency to find work rather than depending on an all but married bartender who I had only hooked up with but who had pimped me out via DVD to find a job.

Yes, I was by now nearing the stone soup portion of my life plan program it seemed.

The Gemini twins were the only people in Portland I had been in contact with; well they were the only people I had been in contact with period, other than my less-than-amused-with-my-behavior family. And the twins had only heard from me by mail. I sent a check for rent with no return address along with a note thanking them for letting me be a part of that happy little household much longer than ANY of us intended and that it was time for me to move on. Meaning I was down on the farm for a yet to be determined time. This was not Bowen or Entertainment Tonight induced. I needed to hibernate and would have to reinvent myself.

I also had to go back to Portland to accomplish that kind of Houdini act, the reinvention of Wyatt. Rome seemed a good place to disappear to and become someone new, perhaps find Mattey, but that was a pipe dream for the moment. After the headlines died down I'd need that cache of cash I had squirreled away in my room in Portland and did NOT want to tempt Janus and Juno by asking them to pack for me and having them find my little pot 'o gold. Our relationships had settled back into an uneasy friendship that would go down faster than the *Costa Concordia* if I gave them the chance to be tempted by my bankroll.

Wiping my hands on my already dirty jeans once the chopper was out of sight, I remounted my tractor and drove home.

Later that night, I jumped when the phone rang. Seeing that it was James, I answered. I missed my snarky friend and by then was even aching a tiny bit for Flora and Fauna; Cold Claire would have gotten a big hug and even stony the driver and Jean the world's most surely chef would have gotten happy greetings from me at that point.

Only William-I-left-my-heart-in-your-tiny-plane-Bowen would not have gotten a hello from me. I did wonder if FTD or Pro Blossom did dirt clod delivery so I could continue my assault.

"Dirt! You threw DIRT at William Bowen!" James snorted with laughter in such a genuine and easy way I could not help but be a little proud.

"It was kinda funny, "I agreed. "He's lucky I didn't pick up a rock. His wouldn't be the only body buried out here in the middle of nowhere," I said ominously, hoping someone at Bowen was transcribing this part of the conversation to Bowen. What was he gonna do, fire me and let me be free to start selling my version of the story? "Why is he telling me shit now?" I was stretched out over the bed; James and I had been gabbing away for nearly half an hour.

"What kinda shit?"

"C'mon, man, you know everything. Don't jerk me around."

"I only know what I have been able to piece together. But I do know he, like, likes you. I TOLD you that. He's got nothing to lose and everything to gain. You. He pays me but now the few friends he had don't trust him and want to distance themselves and now that he is off the board he has nothing to do.

The guys he was doing business with are all
floundering in the same sea of crap he is AND he
isn't bringing them hot ass on the hoof. He knows
for the first time in his life he's effed up royal and for
the first time Daddy isn't there to fix it. He's off the
board and trust me, this will have made all of them
mad enough to try and cut him out of the trust as
well."

There was a pause to let this soak in before
James spoke again.

"He's agreed to help finance the bar."

"Wow, you had the balls to bring that up
NOW?" I admired his style, to get in while Bowen
was down and vulnerable. James had learned well
from the master.

"When I get to Rome I'll put him in for
Sainthood," I deadpanned. I'd told James my big
picture plans because I figured someone other than
the American Embassy should know where I was.

"Seriously, congratulations man."

"Thanks. Are you going to be gone forever?"

"No," I said gloomily, "I have to come back
and get some of my stuff. THEN I'm gonna be gone
forever. Small place like that – no one is ever gonna
forget this. But there have to be drag queens in
Rome and we'll find 'em when you come visit."

"Oh, don't be silly, of course there are drag
queens in Rome and people WILL forget this. It's

just flavor of the moment news and fast enough you and Bowen will be yesterday's attraction. Look, Dahl Baby is having a special change of ownership show in two weeks, then we are shutting down for renovation. You HAVE to be there for that show. Period. Don't make me come back to Little Rock or Capetown or wherever the hell in the sticks you are, because I will. Drag your ass back here with rope and chain if I need to."

"Oh, promises, promises…," I sighed, as we said goodnight and made arrangements for me to come back to the city for the show and to get my few things. I then went back to sweet dreams of tall corn, deep potatoes, and big firm soup stones. I doubted I'd find love on Farmers.com, though, so was glad to be heading to Italy for that extended *Roman Holiday.*

I planned to let the guys I lived with keep the few pieces of furniture in my room so my exit would be lean and smooth. I'd pack, party like a rock star with James, and let my family know where I was once I had landed and ready to start my new life.

Something I was getting sadly adept at even at my young age.

Packing up the small assortment of "city" clothes James had brought to the farm, I had one of my brothers take me to the next village (which I know makes it sound like we are Hobbits but that is what we grew up calling small towns) where I caught a bus (had kinda come full circle huh; arrived by bus, went home by private jet – well part of the way – then back by bus!) to Salem where I rented a car to be returned to the Portland airport. My puzzled, put upon family loved me, but I could tell they were at the same time relieved to have their now somewhat soiled and I am certain kinda creepy wayward son on the move away from home again. They assured me I was always welcome and I promised to keep in touch. I could tell they hoped it would be by phone, cable, telegraph or smoke signal rather than bringing another drama of family shame inducing proportion back home again.

I left with a nearly empty suitcase to be filled with those one or two pieces of my own wardrobe and a fast paced timeline of getting back into Portland laid out that ended with an already ticketed flight to Rome. Where I would find Mattey and see what happened. I had enough money to make it a year or so if I was careful, longer if I found some good soup rocks among the ruins.

Calling Fred and Barney, I made certain the coast was clear of paparazzi around the front of the apartment building, then scooted in through the back door as extra precaution. The Ex-Men greeted me like the long lover/best friend I had been, excitedly chattering that the scandal was the talk in ALL of the clubs, where they of course were getting VIP treatment with no cover charges, free drinks and getting chatted up by all of the hottest guys who all wanted to be hooked up with William Bowen.

They talked while I packed, carefully lifting out the sack of money I had stuck under some shirts in a middle drawer. Their chatter was the perfect diversion as I smoothly stowed the packet of cash away.

Listening to them, I came to realize that despite what had gone on between us, the pain of betrayal and losing someone I thought I loved and someone I had liked as a friend, that these guys were good together. Although it had been to their benefit to let me continue to live there, which made for a better bankroll I now needed in the most desperate of ways, it had been helpful to me as well. They had also brought James to me without question or hesitation. If they could go to those lengths to prove loyalty if not friendship, then there was no reason for me to keep a wall up and keep them out of my life.

Besides, I had bigger targets to hate, like William Bowen.

By the time my small amount of packing was finished, I found myself inviting them to come stay with me when I settled. But I didn't tell them where I was settling, didn't need that spread through the clubs and going on to the media. They were decent guys who had found each other in a pretty rotten way but here at the end of the trail I was happy for all of us.

We hugged all around while I assured them I would be at the club for the show later where we would have a proper round of toasts to send me off to make a new world.

Of course, there was still some bitter before that sweet, though.

Calling James, who was busy moving HIS things out of Rose Bud, he told me to hurry over as Bowen was not home, so I should hurry over to deliver the pieces of Bowen-wear I had at the apartment. You remember I was keeping the socks and underwear as sordid reminders of my time with Bowen. I could have just left them to Zac and Todd, yup, the gruesome two-some have actual names and you are now among those who know them. But by now you know me better than my internist and know that I am adaptable. I was still gonna hold that grudge against William Bowen until Gabriel blew that crazy trumpet, but there was no reason for me to keep holding love against two people I still found myself caring about.

Accidental hooker with a heart of gold, that's me. Think Marsha Mason in *Cinderella Liberty*, *Pretty Woman* by Julia Roberts or *Sweet Charity* ala Shirley McLain. Problem was that everyone had seen too much of me, not just that old "gaynge"of mine, but the world at large and I would give anything to have some of those images back on just the internet and on DVDs where they belonged instead of all over the news.

While I had been assured by James that Bowen would not be at the house, it didn't dawn on me to ask him about photographers lurking about until I slowed to make the turn into that well hidden drive when lightning bolts seemed to be striking me at eye level. What seemed to be an army with cameras surrounded the car. I had at least jammed a ball cap low over my forehead and was wearing Armani shades, but it was hardly in disguise. Aside from the strobe-like flashes, I could hear the camera motors whirring even with the windows up. I could also hear the commentary being yelled by the chasing mob:

"Who is it?"

"Is it him?" I assumed they were looking for Bowen.

Then:

"Wyatt! WYATT, HEY, IT'S WYATT!"

This was not good. With caution, I pressed the gas and moved into the brushy roadway as quickly and carefully as I could, the photographers swarming the back of the car and chasing as I shot toward the small brick guard house. Slamming the brakes on the car was quickly circled by bodies, lights strobing the windows.

Cracking the window as slightly as I could, I called out my name and waited as the cameras flashed. Soon I could see nothing but spots in front of my eyes. The guard, who had been alerted by James, lifted the electronic bar and I slammed my foot to the gas and shot the car through the mob of press. Well, so much for sneaking back in. I'd have to cab or get another ride to the airport. Might even have to change my flight or go to Seattle to get a quiet exit from the Northwest.

Screeching to a halt in front of Rose Bud, I leapt from the car. Shaking from the experience, I grabbed the clothing and dashed in, almost bowled James over.

"What the fuck, man!" he yelped.

"Forgot to warn me about the camera people!" I snarled, throwing the small armload of clothing I held on a chair in the hall. I really wasn't mad at my friend, I'd not thought about them either – hey up until a few weeks earlier I was just a dude doing a job and fucking around a lot, okay?

"Sorry, not mad at YOU."

"Calm down, good to see you, too. You look good," James said, as I moved toward the kitchen, ready to demand something to drink stronger than tea or diet coke. Xanax or black tar heroin wouldn't have calmed me down, but I was willing to give vodka a shot at my nerves.

My hand was on the upper panel of the swinging door leading into the spacious kitchen and I was carping about my exit in when I heard a familiar voice from behind me.

"We're going to have to put me in the trunk of the car to get me out of here," I had just snarled when the other familiar voice broke in behind us.

"What got those photographers all stirred up? Man, they are buzzing like a hive of bees hit with a stick," William Bowen said from the front doorway.

SIXTEEN

Ever have a dream where you are naked in public? Or someplace you should be like an office after hours or as in my case right at that moment in the home of your arch enemy who you thought would not be there?

Biting the inside of my lip, I prayed I tried to wake myself up, hoping the whole thing, start to finish, porn to paparazzi, Rome to Terra Haute would have been a bad dream.

But it wasn't. The smooth wood under my palm was solid and cool, I could smell something baking in the kitchen, and heard Jean slamming things (well some things never changed it seemed) around on the other side of the doorway, blessed feet from where I would love to have been rather than exposed in the hallway with Bowen right behind me. Or on Mars or at the bottom of the ocean in a cool *Nautalis* style submarine, or just under a plain old Marine for that matter. Anywhere but in the front hall of Rose Bud, the most exclusive piece of real estate in Portland, Oregon, owned by my soon-to-be former boss who I'd crushed on, been crushed by, fucked for, and who had most recently been the target of my dirt clod throwing.

My only regret was that I didn't have a piece of dirt in my hand at that very second.

"Good to see you, Wyatt," he said.

Yeah, well, that seemed to be the consensus around there from the photographers who were looking to make a buck or three off my images, to James, and now Bowen. The security guard, a scared looking kid who looked like he was going to wet his pants as the crowd mooshed around my rental car, and Jean were the only two who had not yet weighed in on my appearance.

It was his house, so if Bowen had chosen to uproot one of the orchids in the center of hall table and chuck the debris at me, he would have been within his right. And yeah, I'm just stalling here, hand on the door waiting to see what is going to happen just like you. Kind of like that old game *Mystery Date*, which in this day and age would have had stoners and thugs as part of the behind-the-door rotation and frankly in my crowd they would be more popular than some of the clean scrubbed guys. But that was not the game I was involved in right then. Mine was along the line of seeing how civil I should be to Bowen given what had happened.

But I was raised by good, decent people and this was his home, earned or not, so I turned and said with as much grace as possible, "Thank you, asshole."

Bowen took it well, James suppressed a smirk, and I slammed on into the kitchen with both of them trailing me.

"James, will you and Jean excuse us?" Bowen said, the swinging door not even making a full return with the two of them high tailing it OUT of what was now the danger zone. Bowen moved to the breakfast nook and slid in, eyes locked on me. Fuck, I hated that I still had that hard-on for him. He drug his fingers through his thick, shiny (okay, okay, and sexy) hair and looked up at me. The humbled man sitting at his kitchen table was not the same powerhouse who had been behind the desk at Bowen (and I was so thankful to at least KNOW what Bowen did, at least in part; traffic in human flesh!) or sneering at me in the fast little jet. The man I saw at the table was just that…a guy. A sexy guy in a big house who still had a trust fund as big as the sky to live on even if he no longer had control of his family company, but still a guy.

A guy who had used and abused my trust, too.

"Please?" he said, while nodding toward a chair.

Did I owe him the courtesy of listening to him? No.

But I crossed the room and sat down anyway.

And listened as Bowen opened up with his own movie-of-the-week worthy story. I turned into Father Flannigan at the table as he cited not only his transgressions but those of his forefathers as well.

Minutes turned into hours, hours into the afternoon until James crept quietly back into the kitchen to say he had to leave for the club.

By then Bowen had cried, fuck we both had, and laughed about what he had done as a child to get through his mother's drinking and his father's neglect – the bad choices he had made, the relationships with guys he knew were wrong for him because they were only in it for the money, and the guys he had brought home just to piss everyone off. He talked about watching me; eager, enthusiastic, living with two other people to make ends meet and finally had started to feel bad for the first time about what he was doing because I asked nothing of him and didn't try to use him.

"I'd found a formula that worked, had a string of clients who would give me contracts if I gave them what they wanted, a certain kind of safe and clean guaranteed guy on the side. I knew I was being self destructive and when the board found out, it would be over; kind of my last fuck you to the family, I guess," Bowen sighed, as he drug a finger around the smooth table top.

By then dusk had fallen and I could tell the long confession had drained him; hell, it had drained me.

"This isn't an excuse. You are a great guy, Wyatt, and I'm sorry I didn't see that from the beginning instead of just seeing you as someone who had the look and could fit the suit."

"I'm sorry, too," I said after a long pause. "I knew something was going on but the money kept me in the game. When you have never had it and suddenly do....," I trailed off. Bowen understood.

There was another long silence as we just looked at each other. Fuck, I wish we'd been able to have had this conversation a long time ago.

"What are you going to do?"

I just shrugged rather than tell him my vague plans.

"I won't sell my story if that's what you're worried about."

"No, Wyatt. I do know you better than that," Bowen scoffed.

"Now my ass," I joked, "is another story...."

Bowen laughed and took my hand.

"I really am sorry, Wyatt. You were so cute that first plane ride, holding on for dear life. I'm really not into others suffering but I wanted to throw you down right there in the aisle and do you until we landed."

We both laughed and launched into tales if what the other had really been thinking the last few months, another cathartic conversation that went on until it was full dark outside and I reminded Bowen that we had promised James I would be at the club.

"Me, too. And I have to eat. Starving," Bowen said, his brilliant smile making him even sexier. "Since we are both going to the club, let's have some food and go together."

I wasn't relishing getting through the gauntlet of photographers alone or being stuffed into a trunk, so I agreed. Together Bowen and I grilled salmon we foraged from the refrigerator, tossed a salad and found some asparagus spears lurking in the freezer, so had a balanced meal while making small talk that did not involve the scandal. He was easy to talk to once that fortress of a wall around his heart had been pierced.

After the casual, relaxed meal, he helped me put my bags in the car and we took a little used side road to exit the estate, avoiding the waiting press.

The club was packed and the show in full swing by the time we arrived, but our names were on THE door list so we were led to a front table and squeezed in. James as Jimmie stepped onto the small stage just as we were settled in. I thought his eyes were going to pop out of his lashes when he saw his backer and friend sitting together at the same table.

We left after the show, finding and hugging Zac and Todd, then Jimmie, thanking him for the seats. The drag queen's eyebrows arched nearly to the back of his skull when he realized Bowen and I were not only speaking civilly to each other but leaving together.

"You better call the second you land," he whispered, while holding me in as close as his fake chest would allow.

"Promise," I gulped, a fist size lump suddenly forming in my throat as I realized how much I was going to miss James. I was Dorothy leaving Oz to his Scarecrow.

"Where can I take you?" Bowen asked, as we got into the car.

"Airport, I have an early flight."

"Bullshit," he said, while turning the engine over.

"No, I mean it. Just because we are being all friendly now doesn't mean you are still the boss of me," I grinned.

"Look, the plane is being serviced. In the morning I'll have the pilot take you anywhere you want to go. Anywhere."

There was a silence as Bowen pulled into traffic.

"But I would prefer it if you would come home. With me. It'll be easier to be pariahs if we are together, and Rose Bud has plenty of room."

"Look, I just don't think," I started, as Bowen pulled back out of traffic and into a grocery lot, easing the big car between the white lines of a parking space.

"Then don't think," Bowen said, as he leaned in, "just kiss me."

So I did.

SIX MONTHS LATER

I hadn't gotten on the little plane the next morning.

After some serious making out there in the least romantic spot in the universe, a Safeway parking lot scattered with paper scraps, bottles, cans, one of the hottest guys I'd ever locked lips with made out like it was the only thing making our hearts beat. After the kissing it didn't take that much effort for Bowen to get me to come back to Rose Bud to talk (and make out...) some more. After all, at that point I really wasn't an official Bowen Industries employee any more.

The conversation, talking and confessing and getting to know each other went on for several days as he convinced me to stay on at Rose Bud for awhile as a guest. While we still might not have agreed with each other on everything, one thing we knew for certain was that I was going to be unemployable for a while unless I went to Amsterdam or put up an ad on Craigslist offering massage under "Therapeutic Massage."

But employment or lack of employment was not why I stayed. Yes, I was always attracted to Bowen, but as I got to really know him I started to like him, too. Without needing to keep up a force field made up of equal parts mean and powerful to keep people (parents, friends, boyfriends, board of directors), Bill for the first time in his life got to be human. He was funny with a sly wit and in certain areas refreshingly stupid, knowing nothing about art, literature or even the politicians he had been influencing. So yeah, eventually I moved out of the guest room and into the master suite some time after that long first night of talking.

The photographers had long left the hill in search of newer, fresher material. Bill and I had no trouble coming and going and the greenhorn in the guard station had matured into an excellent security force, putting in long, boring hours for which we made certain he was well paid.

Yes, the former boss and I had become a couple and while I had been able to forgive him, I could tell it was going to be a while before he forgave himself for what had happened. My initial lust for him, followed by fear, then hate, had never wavered and it turned out he had developed quite a Jones for yours truly as well.

The club reopened with a huge fanfare. Two local television stations covered it, and queens from

Vancouver to San Francisco came in for the event. Business was booming. James even hired Zac and Todd as servers and they were raking in the tips after some snark training from yours truly.

The suits were all given to charity; well, all the clothes but the underwear and socks which I did keep, were given away, and I was slowly rebuilding my own collection. Bill was planning a trip to Rome for us where we would see the city and the tailor. And, of course, we would find Mattey for proper apologies to him.

Do leopards change their spots? No, but they can be made into coats, and I wore Bowen like a ¾ length evening jacket. Bill was still a work in progress and I made it clear that if he pushed me, effed me over and didn't put some effort into what we were going to do, that I was outa there. He could be spoiled, willful and got angry quickly, but a hard stare from me could take him down. He was a challenge, yeah, but he was my challenge.

We were hosting a little dinner party, our first as a couple, so I was fussing around the large living room plumping pillows and adjusting floral arrangements. Bill was right; it was nice to be doing this together. We were a couple of lone wolves together now. On the mantel I pushed a silver framed photo of Zac and Todd back slightly, adjusted a framed photo of James in high drag, then picked up a framed shot of Bill and me. We'd come a long way since the day of my Bowen interview, charade that it was. But now we'd found each other and after the crap we had just lived through, we knew we could make it stick. I still had a song from *A Chorus Line* running through my head, only it was the act two closer, that sweet ballad *What I did for love* that I now found myself usually humming to myself absently.

"*Kiss today goodbye, the sweetness and the sorrow, wish me luck the same to you-and I won't forget what I did for love, what I did for love....*"

Putting the frame back, I smiled at the rock.

Yup. I wasn't taking any chances. The first morning after Bill and I had slept together I got up early and went to the garden, and finding a good size smooth stone I brought it in, washed it down, and now it sat on the mantel. Bill would always have Rose Bud and the trust fund and while I had put away that nice little nest egg that was growing with investments every day, you just never knew when you would need a pot and some water, someone to love, and a soup sized stone for two to get by.

THE END

ABOUT THE AUTHOR

James Brock spent his childhood on a homestead in central Alaska with no electricity, indoor plumbing or running water. Reading by oil lamp was the family hobby, with James quickly moving from *The Bobbsey Twins* and *The Boxcar Children* to Dorothy Parker and Robert Benchley.

Stories by James have been published in many gay magazines, and writing featured in *The Seattle Standard*, *The Seattle Gay News*, along with two Alyson Publication anthologies. He has sold comedy material to Joan Rivers and Phyllis Diller and his novel ***Men Overboard!***, a comic murder mystery set on an all gay cruise, is available on Amazon. His first gay romance, ***Panda Heart***, can be found at Beau to Beau publishing.

James lives in Seattle where he enjoys running water and warm porcelain.

This print book is also available in ebook form from the following:

Amazon Kindle Stores

Barnes & Noble

Apple iBookstores

Sony Reader Store

Rainbow ebooks

All Romance ebooks

Romance Novel Store

1 Place for Romance

Bookstrand

Coffeetime Romance